CAR]    [

MW00695209

"Easily the craziest, weirdest, strangest, funniest, most obscene writer in America."
—*GOTHIC MAGAZINE*

"Carlton Mellick III has the craziest book titles... and the kinkiest fans!"
—CHRISTOPHER MOORE, author of *The Stupidest Angel*

"If you haven't read Mellick you're not nearly perverse enough for the twenty first century."
—JACK KETCHUM, author of *The Girl Next Door*

"Carlton Mellick III is one of bizarro fiction's most talented practitioners, a virtuoso of the surreal, science fictional tale."
—CORY DOCTOROW, author of *Little Brother*

"Bizarre, twisted, and emotionally raw—Carlton Mellick's fiction is the literary equivalent of putting your brain in a blender."
—BRIAN KEENE, author of *The Rising*

"Carlton Mellick III exemplifies the intelligence and wit that lurks between its lurid covers. In a genre where crude titles are an art in themselves, Mellick is a true artist."
—*THE GUARDIAN*

"Just as Pop had Andy Warhol and Dada Tristan Tzara, the bizarro movement has its very own P. T. Barnum-type practitioner. He's the mutton-chopped author of such books as *Electric Jesus Corpse* and *The Menstruating Mall*, the illustrator, editor, and instructor of all things bizarro, and his name is Carlton Mellick III."
—*DETAILS MAGAZINE*

Also by
Carlton Mellick III

SPIDER
BUNNY

CARLTON MELLICK III

ERASERHEAD PRESS
PORTLAND, OREGON

ERASERHEAD PRESS
205 NE BRYANT
PORTLAND, OR 97211

WWW.ERASERHEADPRESS.COM

ISBN: 978-1-62105-231-9

AUTHOR'S NOTE

I was an '80s kid. This means I was raised on a whole lot of weird ass shit. Our cartoons, our toys, our movies, our music, our clothing styles—everything was a massive collection of what the fuck. In fact, I believe the creation of the bizarro fiction genre had everything to do with the impact the '80s had on children. Many of the leading bizarro fiction writers were born in 1977. Jeremy Robert Johnson, Kevin L. Donihe, Chris Genoa, G. Arthur Brown, and I were all born that year, just a few months apart. So our entire childhoods, from ages 3 to 13, were influenced by that decade. And I'm pretty sure it completely, irreversibly warped our brains forever.

But it was not the typical, memorable things about the '80s that had the biggest influence on us. It was all the long forgotten stuff—the songs, the cartoons, the television shows, the commercials that hardly anyone remembers. Our cartoons weren't just Transformers, Smurfs and Thundercats. It was Kidd Video, Galaxy High School and Hulk Hogan's Rock 'N' Wrestling. Our music wasn't just Talking Heads, Cindi Lauper, and Devo, it was also this weird electro bubblegum pop that was only played at roller skating rinks that I haven't heard of since. And the commercials… man, the commercials. There was some weird ass shit going on in those commercials. Shit that often gave me nightmares.

There was this one commercial that especially disturbed me. It was for a cereal called Circus Fun. I remember the commercial vividly. The mascot for the cereal was this creepy Claymation clown. It would appear under the bed of these two children, waking them up and beckoning them toward the breakfast table. The children would get all excited about the clown under their bed, even though the logical reaction would have been one of batshit terror. The clown would then conjure up a line of circus animals, all terribly claymated in horrific ways, which also came out from under the children's beds and marched one by one into their cereal bowls. As a kid, this commercial freaked the hell out of me. I was terrified that I would find strange claymated clowns hiding in my bedroom.

I had forgotten all about it for years until I was in my early twenties. When I remembered the Circus Fun commercial, I asked all my friends about it. But nobody knew what the hell I was talking about. Not only had they never seen the commercials, but they never even heard of the cereal before. I went online and researched Circus Fun and there was no mention of it anywhere. It was like the cereal and the commercial never existed. All of this made the memory a hell of a lot creepier.

After reading the Creepypasta story *Candle Cove*—about a terrifying children's show that nobody remembers—it made me think of my experience with the Circus Fun commercial and inspired me to write this book. I'm a big fan of this kind of story. It was a lot of fun to write. Like my last three books, this one started as a short story that mutated into a novella because I was enjoying it too much to let it end. I hope you like it.

By the way, upon writing this, I looked up Circus Fun online once again and it turns out that it did actually exist. There's now plenty of information about it and one of the commercials is even on youtube. I still have yet to meet anyone who remembers it, but at least I didn't dream up the whole thing.

—Carlton Mellick III 9/26/2016 9:34pm

CHAPTER
ONE

It's been days since we've been trapped inside the cereal commercial. I'm not sure how many days. Dave says that it's been twelve, but there's really no way to be sure. It's only morning here. Always morning. Outside the kitchen window, the canary-yellow sun never moves from its spot, just frozen in the sky like it was painted onto a massive billboard.

We're all exhausted, sitting on the tile floor, leaning against the cabinets and the refrigerator door. Peri has her hair in her face, rocking back and forth, trying to block out the hideous children sitting at the breakfast table. I try to comfort her, but she won't let me touch her, won't even look at me. She blames me for bringing them here. They all blame me.

"What are we going to do?" Kim asks.

Dave shrugs. It's the same question she's been asking for days. Nobody has an answer for her, but she keeps on asking anyway.

"I have no idea," Dave says.

Kim shakes her head at his response. "There has

to be a way out. We can't just give up."

On the other side of the kitchen, a group of hideous children sit around the breakfast table, eating large bowls of Fruit Fun cereal. There are four of them, ranging from ages three to ten, each one more grotesque than the last. They were animated cartoon characters when we watched them on television in the real world. But ever since we entered the commercial, their cartoon forms became flesh. Their chunky cheeks filled with cereal. Plump lips curled in permanent smiles. Their beady little eyes spread too far apart on their faces.

They never pay us any attention. They just eat their cereal in silence, every once in a while talking about how delicious it is or how Fruit Fun is an important part of a balanced breakfast. They speak in high-pitched chipmunk voices that don't seem to sync up with their moving lips. I've never seen them get up from the table. It's like their bodies are fused to the white wood chairs.

"If there was a way in, there has to be a way out," I tell them.

They both glare at me with bloodshot eyes. They don't want to hear a word that comes out of my mouth, not unless I've figured a way to get them back home. I understand why they're so angry and frustrated. They've had very little sleep and have been eating nothing but milk and sugary cereal. They don't know if they'll ever see their families again. I wish there was something I could say that would comfort them, something that would inspire them not to give up hope.

But I have no idea what that would be. I feel like I've damned us all.

"I don't want to die here," Kim says to her boyfriend.

Dave hugs her close to him, brushes the tears from her eyes.

Kim calms down, releasing her weight into his arms, but then the sound of an opening door tenses her right back up. Floppy footsteps echo through the foyer.

Their eyes widen and shiver.

"She's here…" Kim says in a trembling voice.

"Hide!" Dave cries, crawling to his feet.

We rush to our hiding spots. Kim and Dave crawl into the empty cabinets, Peri squeezes herself into the refrigerator, and I hide behind the curtains. My hiding spot leaves me the most exposed, but there's just no place else to go.

I can see her entering the kitchen through the fabric of the curtain. She walks with big fuzzy feet, bouncing with each step. Her long bunny ears droop past her bare shoulders. Her big, bulging cartoon eyes twitch and curl inside of their sockets. She doesn't wear clothes. Her skin is pink and white with purple polka dots. A fluffy tail wiggles against her pink butt. Her whiskers stand up on end as she smiles at the children eating the breakfast she brings them.

She's Berry Bunny, the mascot of Fruit Fun cereal, the lord of this domain. I have no idea where she came from or what she really is. All I know is that if we want to survive, we must stay far, far away from her.

CHAPTER
TWO

It all started with a conversation...

"Who's your favorite cereal mascot?" Dave asked.

We were sitting in our dorm room with our girlfriends, drinking cheap beer, just bullshitting and avoiding our German homework.

"Like Trix the rabbit or Tony the Tiger?" Kim asked.

"Yeah," he said. "Which one is your favorite?"

Kim thought about it for a minute. She sat on my bed while painting her toenails, getting gold nail polish all over my bedspread, too drunk to really care.

"Probably Toucan Sam," she said. "From Fruit Loops."

"What?" Dave seemed almost offended by her answer. "Why the hell would you like Toucan Sam?"

Kim shrugged. "Fruit Loops was my favorite cereal when I was a kid."

"I didn't ask you what your favorite cereal was," Dave said. "I wanted to know your favorite mascot. Which character did you like best?"

"I already told you. Fruit Loops was my favorite cereal so Toucan Sam was my favorite mascot."

Dave just dismissed his girlfriend with a wave of his hand. "Fine. Toucan Sam." Then he looked at me. "What about you, Pete?"

I took a swig of beer. "The Smacks frog maybe. My favorite cereal was Apple Jacks but they didn't really have a mascot."

"Dig'em Frog? Seriously? Who the hell likes the Dig'em Frog? Man you guys are all boring."

"Cap'n Crunch then," I said. "I don't know."

"Well, which mascot did you like best?" Kim asked him.

"Who do you think?"

I shrugged at him. "Lucky?"

"No, not Lucky. Fuck that pussy leprechaun."

"Then who?" Kim asked.

"Sugar Bear," Dave said. "Duh."

"Sugar Bear?" I asked.

"Hell yeah, Sugar Bear," he said, pumping his fist in the air. "Sugar Bear was the man!"

"Who's Sugar Bear?" Kim asked.

"You know, from Super Golden Crisp. He's only the coolest cereal mascot of all time."

Peri was silent, sitting on my lap in the most uncomfortable way possible. She was deep in thought, trying to figure out which mascot she liked best.

Then she asked, "How come there aren't any female cereal mascots?"

"There's female cereal mascots," Dave said.

"No, there's not," Kim said. "It's totally sexist."

"There has to be," he said.

"Name one."

Dave scanned his brain, trying to think of one. I thought about it as well. I could have sworn I'd seen female cereal mascots in the past.

"The bee from Honey Nut Cheerios?" Dave asked.

Kim shook her head. "That's a boy, too."

Dave let out a frustrated groan and set his beer down. "I have to look this up."

He opened his laptop and googled female cereal mascots, but didn't come up with anything.

"I think you're right," he said. "There's never been a female cereal mascot. That's fucked up."

"No, I think I remember one…" I told them.

They looked at me.

"Which one?" Dave asked.

Then the memory came back to me. A cereal commercial I hadn't thought about in years.

"Berry Bunny," I said.

"Who?" Kim asked.

"From that cereal… what was it called…" Then the memory came back. "Fruit Fun."

They looked at me like I was crazy.

Dave asked, "Fruit Fun? What the fuck is Fruit Fun?"

I said, "You know, Fruit Fun. You've never had it before?"

They all shook their heads. When I thought about it, I realized I had never had it myself. I'd never even seen it in the stores.

"The commercials used to be on television all the time when I was a kid," I said.

14

I remembered the commercials clearly. The kids gathered around the breakfast table and a little cartoon bunny girl would come into the kitchen and give them all bowls of colorful cereal.

"She was the pink bunny with purple polka dots. You don't remember?"

They just brushed me off.

"You're fucking with us," Kim said.

"No, I'm serious."

"There's no such thing."

Dave looked it up online. There was no mention of a Berry Bunny or a Fruit Fun cereal.

"I'm not making it up," I told them. "I swear."

But they wouldn't hear it. They just assumed I was messing with them.

Later that night, I went online to search for myself. I wondered if I'd gotten the name of the cereal wrong. Perhaps it was Fruit Flakes or Berry Buns. But nothing came up in any google search. I searched for "bunny cereal mascot" and "fruit cereal" but I only got links to Trix and Fruit Loops. I even watched YouTube clips of old cereal commercials and read articles about kids' cereals that no longer exist. Nothing came up.

Part of me wondered if all of it was a false memory. Perhaps there never was a Fruit Fun cereal. Perhaps it was just something I saw in an old movie or in a dream.

Maybe it was just something my brain made up on the spot. I wasn't sure. I didn't remember when or where I saw the commercials. I just knew that it was a very long time ago.

After I went to sleep, I dreamt about watching Fruit Fun commercials. I was a child watching television in the family room, sitting on the floor in my pajamas, surrounded by action figures. Berry Bunny came on the screen holding up a bowl of Fruit Fun. She was a six year old girl with floppy bunny ears and a fluffy tail.

"It's always a fun time with Fruit Fun," the bunny said, holding up her bowl. That was the catch phrase. It was what Berry Bunny always said in every commercial.

I couldn't make out what the cereal actually looked like. It was a cartoon, so the cereal was just a bowlful of bright pink shapeless lumps. The bunny looked down into the cereal bowl, eating it with an overly large spoon.

"You're absolutely delicious," she said to the cereal. The sound of her voice was high-pitched and squeaky. It made my skin crawl.

She licked her whiskers after every bite, moaning deep satisfaction as though she was eating the greatest food imaginable. "Nothing beats a bowl of Fruit Fun."

But then I got a good look inside the bowl. The commercial showed the contents of the cereal in a close-up shot. It was no longer just a bowl of shapeless pink lumps. The bowl was filled with crying children. They were either naked or they wore pink clothes, swimming in a pool of pink milk.

Berry Bunny devoured each of the miniature children one spoonful at a time, swallowing them whole. The children screamed in terror, begging not to be eaten. But the cartoon bunny ate every single one of them. When she was finished, she laid back in a chair rubbing her swollen belly, a satisfied smile on her face.

Just before the commercial ended, a female announcer's voice said, "Fruit Fun—a belly full of fun."

When I woke up covered in sweat, memories flooded into my head. I remembered it. All of it. That wasn't a dream. It was a memory. I clearly remembered seeing that commercial as a kid and it horrified me. It used to give me nightmares. The frightened look on the children's faces were so real, like the children were really being eaten alive. I had no idea why they would make such a horrific commercial for a kid's cereal.

But the thing that really confused me was why nobody else had ever seen the commercial before. Was it so shocking that parents had it pulled from the air? Were the commercials destroyed, never to be shown again? Did all the children who'd seen those commercials block it from their memories as well? I had no idea. But one thing I knew: despite the fact that they weren't mentioned anywhere on the internet, these commercials were definitely real.

I couldn't sleep for the rest of the night. Every time I closed my eyes, I saw the image of Berry Bunny eating bowls of crying children. She licked her whiskers and glared at me through the television screen, watching me with her big cartoon eyes.

In German class the next day, I tried to tell Peri about my dream.

"Vas hast du getraumen?" Peri asked.

As a serious student, she only spoke German during German class. I tried to explain my dream to her, but my German was terrible.

"Ich hab getraumte…" But after three words I decided to go back to my normal tongue. "Well, it was a nightmare about something I saw when I was a kid."

"Deutsch sprechen."

But I didn't know how to explain my nightmare in German. I'd taken three years of it and still didn't know a tenth of what the classes have covered. Languages have never been my strong suit. I thought I would have had an easy time with German, since both of my fathers were from Germany and spoke their native language fluently. I, on the other hand, had a hard enough time with English, let alone German.

"Ich hatte…" Then I shook my head. "Look, I just want to talk about my dream."

Peri gave up on me. In an annoyed tone, she asked, "Fine. What dream?"

"It was a memory. A flashback of a commercial I saw when I was a kid that used to give me nightmares."

"A commercial?"

"That cereal commercial. The one I mentioned last night. Fruit Fun cereal."

"You weren't actually making that up?"

"No, I vividly remember those commercials as a kid."

Peri took the horn-rimmed glasses off of her face and cleaned them with her shirt as she said, "But Dave said they don't exist. They're not on the internet."

"Just because they aren't mentioned on the internet doesn't mean they don't exist. I know they're real. They used to give me nightmares."

Then I told her all about the dream I had. I told her about Berry Bunny eating the screaming children, about all the horrible dreams I had after watching them, about how they were so traumatic for a six-year-old boy that I must have blocked them out.

"Are you sure you didn't just make them up? You were only six. They could be false memories. Or they could have been reoccurring nightmares you had as a kid."

"Maybe..." I looked away from her. "But they seem so real. I remember every last detail of these memories. Dreams aren't like that."

"Perhaps you should see a therapist," she said. "There might be a reason you blocked out these memories."

I shook my head. "I don't know... I don't think so..."

I didn't like the idea of seeing a therapist. My parents took me to one when I was in high school, at a time when I was depressed a lot, but it wasn't a very good experience. I didn't like talking about my personal problems. Being fifteen at the time, my problems seemed embarrassing and trivial: kids bullied me, girls didn't like me, everyone thought I was homosexual

19

because of the way I spoke—my fathers were both German immigrants with strong gay lisps and I picked up their accents as a child, constantly getting teased for it. Because I had no friends, I spent most of my time just smoking pot and playing video games. My parents were always worried about my anti-social behavior and tried to do whatever they could to help me out. But that only made things worse. When the other kids found out I was in therapy it only gave them more ammunition to attack me with.

These days, my life is much different. I have a girlfriend. I have friends. I like most of my classes. I don't have to live with my parents. Therapy would be the last thing I'd want to have to deal with.

But I still wanted to know where the heck those commercials came from. I had to know whether they were real or just in my head.

Peri and I went on a date after class. We had a tradition of taking each other on horrible dates. It was a contest we had to see who could come up with the worst possible date to take the other on. The first one I chose was to dress up like we were going to prom, only to eat dinner at Hardee's and drink cans of Steel Reserve in the parking lot. Then we made out while blasting White Lion power ballads on my car stereo.

It was her turn to decide that night and she took

us to Christian Karaoke where she forced me to sing Christian rock songs as passionately as I could, even though I'd never heard of the bands before. It was kind of an unfair choice, since she actually knew the words to a lot of the music. Her parents were hardcore Christians and bought her a lot of Christian rock mp3s when she was young. Some of the songs she could sing perfectly.

When I went up, standing in front of the group of Christian college kids who put this event on every Thursday night in the Rec Center, none of them knowing who the hell I was, I sang a song called *Just Say Jesus* because the title sounded so cheesy. I thought it would be a funny song but it turned out to be a very serious, uplifting rock ballad. It also turned out to be a song many members of the audience loved. They were not too happy to hear me butcher the song, singing it in an almost mocking tone.

When I sat down, I covered my face with my hands and Peri laughed at me. She was really getting a kick out of seeing me embarrass myself.

"You're evil," I told her.

"Did I win?" she asked. "Is this the worst date ever?"

I shook my head. "It's brutal, but I'm not giving up yet. Just wait until next week. You're going to regret taking me to Christian Karaoke."

She smiled. "Oh no… What have I done…"

But then she just laughed. I couldn't tell her what I had planned. It had to be a surprise. But I had a triple threat in store for her. We'd start off with a picnic in

21

a trailer park where we'd eat cans of Vienna sausage, processed cheese slices wrapped around Carl Budding lunchmeat, jars of apricot baby food, and fuzzy navel wine coolers. Then I'd tell her that I signed her up for a Steampunk costume contest and she'd have to wear an extra embarrassing costume I made myself out of tin foil, cardboard, and old concert t-shirts. At the end of the night, I'd take her back to my dorm room and put on a clown porn video—which wasn't only supposed to be one of the trashiest, most revolting porn videos online, but her fear of clowns would make it extra appalling for her.

Perhaps my plan was a little mean, but the rule was that you had to do whatever the other person had planned no matter what it was. If you refused then you lost the game. Peri was the kind of person who wanted to win everything, no matter what the contest, so I'm sure she'd give it a shot. But if anything would make her throw in the towel it would be clown porn.

"I'm having fun," Peri said, stirring her vodka-spiked grape juice.

"You're not supposed to have fun," I said. "These dates are meant to make each other miserable."

She shrugged with a smile on her purple lips. "It's my date. I can have fun as much as I want to, just as long as you don't."

"You're loving watching me cringe, aren't you?"

She just took another sip of her juice in response.

"We should invite Dave and Kim," she said, digging her phone out of her purse. "They'd think

22

this is hilarious."

"It's our date," I said. "You can't invite anyone else."

But she texted them anyway. "It'll be a double date."

That was the only problem with dating Peri. She always wanted to bring Dave and Kim along to everything, even when it was during our bad date contest. Whenever it was her turn, she always wanted to share her bad date with other people. Torturing me alone wasn't enough. She had to bring others along with us, so they could laugh at my humiliation, even though she didn't force them to do the embarrassing things that I had to do.

It only took a few minutes before she got a response.

"Dave's coming," she said.

"Dave? What about Kim?"

She just shrugged.

Dave showed up forty minutes later in a Darth Vader outfit. He had a part time job where he dressed up as Darth Vader for kid's birthday parties, so he could often be seen walking around campus dressed as the Sith Lord. Unfortunately, it made everyone think he was a cosplay nerd even though he only dressed that way for work. He didn't even like Star Wars.

All the Christian kids stared at him as he walked into the room, wondering what the hell Darth Vader was doing at Christian Karaoke. Dave just ignored everyone as he sat down at our table. He took his mask off and wiped sweat from his shaved head.

"Man, I hate kids," he said, dropping the helmet on the table so loudly it interrupted the girl on the Karaoke stage.

"Then why work with them?" Peri asked, giggling.

"For money," he said.

"Why don't you do something else?" she asked, handing him her pint of vodka beneath the table. "They're hiring at my work right now. I could talk to my boss."

He didn't try to be inconspicuous while drinking from the liquor bottle.

"At Baskin and Robbins?" He finished off the rest of the bottle, even though it wasn't his. It wasn't even Peri's to offer. "Fuck that. Only losers work in ice cream shops."

Peri giggled at his words even though he was being rude to her.

I knew my girlfriend had a crush on my roommate. She always had. In fact, I'm pretty sure she only dated me because she was trying to get closer to Dave, hoping that he'd eventually break up with Kim and then she'd be in a good position to make a move. She was just that kind of person. And Dave was just the kind of person who wouldn't have a problem taking his best friend's girlfriend. He did it before. His current girlfriend, Kim, was my girlfriend before she was his. She was in my Rhetoric class and we used to flirt with each other all the time. Then we hooked up at a party and dated for a couple of weeks. But one day, the first time she slept over at my dorm, she woke up in my bed and saw my roommate doing pushups on his side of the room. She fell for him immediately. A couple of days later, they were in a relationship and I had to deal with it. I had to watch her sleeping in my roommate's bed every night and the both of them pretended that our relationship never even happened.

For about a month, it was difficult putting up with them as a couple. But then I met Peri in German class and we hit it off right away. It wasn't serious at first, but we spent a lot of time together. When she met Dave, she obviously was into him. She flirted with him as much as she could whenever Kim wasn't around. Dave always embraced the flirtation.

I didn't understand why girls always chose Dave over me. I'm a much more attractive guy. I have nicer hair, nicer clothes, a nicer face and next to no body fat. But Dave is more confident, more masculine, more athletic, and even though he treats a lot of people like shit, he tends to be a lot of fun to be around. He's just the kind of guy people look up to. That's not who I am.

"You're up next," Peri told me, pushing the laminated list of karaoke songs to me.

I looked up at her. "Me? Again?"

She nodded. "I chose this one just for you."

"Why don't we give Dave a turn?" I asked. "He should do it."

When I said that, Peri gave me a dirty look, annoyed

that I wouldn't leave the table so that they could be by themselves.

"Fuck that," Dave said. "I'm not doing this shit."

The Christians at the next table looked over at Dave when he said that.

The DJ called my name to the stage.

"Try not to laugh too hard," I told them, as I got to my feet, expecting to make an ass out of myself in front of them.

It was one thing to embarrass myself in front of Peri, but the thought of both Peri and Dave sitting together laughing at me as I sang a Christian rock song was going to be so much worse.

Only they didn't laugh at me. They didn't even look at me as I got on stage. As I sang the song, I didn't put any effort into it at all. I just read the words on the monitor, my voice hardly intelligible. I watched Dave and Peri sitting together, talking, laughing. Dave had his hand on her leg. She looked like she was having a better time with him on our date than she was with me.

As I sang the song, I saw something pink in the corner of my eye. I looked to the right, but there was nothing there. I continued reading the lyrics. Just reading, not singing. Then I saw another flash of pink. Something in the back of the room, hopping behind members of the audience. Then I heard high-pitched giggles echo behind my ear. I could swear it was Berry Bunny from the Fruit Fun commercials. But by the time the song was done, there was no sign of the cartoon rabbit. It was all in my head.

Maybe Peri was right. Maybe I did need to see a therapist.

The whole walk back to the dorms, Peri was practically arm in arm with Dave. She hung on his every word, laughed at his every joke, pretending just for a moment that he was her boyfriend instead of Kim's. I followed behind them, kicking rocks and crushed beer cans, listening to Dave rant about his favorite UFC competitors. When Peri said goodbye to us, she gave Dave a quick hug and then grabbed me, kissed me deeply, her tongue shoved down my throat. For a second, I thought my jealousy was unfounded, that her flirtation was innocent and meant nothing, that she really cared only for me. But then I realized she wasn't kissing me for my sake. She was kissing me in front of Dave to make him jealous, to show him what he's missing.

When she left, she didn't say anything to me. She just kissed me, then said goodbye to Dave and walked away.

Before Dave went to bed that night, I told him, "Touch

my girlfriend and I'm going to strangle you in your sleep."

Dave freaked out after I said that. He didn't know where the hell it was coming from.

"What?" he cried, standing up out of bed. "What did you just say to me?"

I rolled over and closed my eyes. "Just stay away from Peri."

He didn't deny anything. He just said, "Don't you fucking threaten me. I'll destroy you."

He took my backpack from my desk and threw it at me. Books and papers exploded across the room. I didn't move or say another word. There's no way I could beat Dave in a fight, but I had to let him know that I wouldn't let him get away with taking another girlfriend from me. At least I wouldn't give her up without a fuss like I did with Kim. I couldn't let the guy walk all over me and just sit there and take it.

The asshole grumbled in his bed for the next hour, laying in the dark, cursing at me with unintelligible words. I knew Dave. He'd been my roommate and best friend for the past few years. He knew that Peri liked him. And because he knew that, it wouldn't be long before he tried to have sex with her. Even though he's with Kim, if the opportunity presented itself he wouldn't hesitate for a second. He cheated on Kim several times already, almost every time she went home to visit her family or whenever she decided to skip a keg party to do homework. And he's even less loyal to his friends than his girlfriends. He's the

28

kind of guy who thinks he's entitled to everything he wants and there's no consequences to his actions. Even though he's my best friend, I absolutely loathe the guy sometimes.

CHAPTER
THREE

That night, another memory came back to me in the form of a dream. I was a year or so older than I was the last time. Seven or eight. I was drawing pictures with my new art set that my fathers bought me for my birthday, watching an episode of Pokémon on Cartoon Network, when a Fruit Fun commercial came on the air.

My skin crawled the second I heard Berry Bunny's high-pitched voice. The hair on my head stood up. It had been a long time since I'd seen a Fruit Fun commercial. I'd almost forgotten about them.

I didn't look up at the television as the commercial ran, keeping my eyes on my drawing, trying to block out the sound.

"Take a bite of my Fruit Fun cereal," Berry Bunny said to a group of four cartoon children, gathered around a breakfast table. "It's berry delicious!"

My hands were shaking as I drew my picture. The lines of the house became wavy scribbles.

"Thanks, Berry Bunny!" said one of the children. "Your cereal is the best!"

I heard cereal pouring into bowls and the children eating their breakfast with delight.

"Yummy!" cried the little girl. "I love how it wiggles down my throat!"

When the girl said that, I glanced up at the television. The little girl's bowl wasn't filled with cereal. It was filled with miniature children, screaming and crying, swimming inside of the pink milk. The cartoon children ate the mini people like ordinary cereal, as though they were just Fruit Loops or Frosted Flakes.

"I like the sound it makes when I eat it!" said another child, the oldest boy, who put his ear to the cereal and listened to the tiny people's cries as if they were making the snap-crackle-popping noise of Rice Crispies.

Then the older girl said, "I like how each piece of Fruit Fun cereal begs for mercy right before you eat it!"

Another child said, "I like how they scream in terror when you pick them up with your spoon!"

The smallest child said, "I like how they shriek in agony when you chew them in your mouth!"

As I watched the commercial, my eyes were frozen in shock. I wanted to look away, but I just couldn't. How was this a cereal commercial for children? Blood and intestines dribbled down the children's mouths. A freshly severed head plopped onto the table like a stray pea. A girl picked bones out of her teeth with a toothpick. It didn't make sense. If this was a real commercial what were they trying to sell? It was too gruesome, too disgusting.

Then Berry Bunny came on the screen. She looked

at the children, hopping with glee, happy that they were enjoying her cereal.

"And remember, Fruit Fun isn't just tasty, it's good for you, too!" she told them. "With over thirteen vitamins and minerals, it's an important part of a balanced breakfast."

Berry Bunny looked different to me. She was older. Just a couple years older. Eight or nine, like me. Before she was barely able to reach the breakfast table, but now she was tall. She was thinner with less baby fat. I didn't understand why they'd change the age and appearance of their mascot, but Berry Bunny had definitely aged since the last time I'd seen the last Fruit Fun commercial.

The commercial went on for several minutes. Far, far longer than an average commercial. It just continued, the children eating the bowls of tiny people, the bunny girl smiling and hopping with excitement, the screams of terror coming from their spoons. The camera angle didn't change.

For five more minutes, the commercial continued, but there wasn't any talking. The children just continued eating, gobbling down mini-child after mini-child, the sound of grunting and smacking, slurping and moaning. I wanted to turn the television off, but I couldn't find the remote. I could have turned it off manually, but that would mean getting too close to the television screen, too close to the commercial.

After staring at her for a full minute, Berry Bunny turned and looked directly at me. She smiled.

"How about you, Petey?" she asked me. "Do you want to try my Fruit Fun cereal?"

My heart nearly stopped. She could see me. She knew my name.

"Have a bite," she said.

She held out a spoonful of her cereal. Her arm went through the television screen into my living room, stretching as far as she could reach. On my side of the screen, her arm was no longer a cartoon. It was real. Her pink and purple skin glistened with sweat. Her red fingernails like claws.

And inside the spoon, I saw three miniature children. They were human. The same age as me. When they saw me, they waved their arms and hopped up and down, trying to get my attention.

"Help us!" one of them cried. "Get us out of the commercial!"

A miniature girl screamed, "They're going to eat us!"

I backed away from the spoon before it could get too close to my face, scrambled over my artwork to the back of the room.

"Don't want any?" asked Berry Bunny. "Fine. Suit yourself."

Then she put the spoonful of children in her mouth. She swallowed them with a loud gulp and then let out a sigh of satisfaction.

"More for me," she said.

After that, I ran out of there and went into my fathers' room, screaming in horror. They had no idea what was wrong with me. I was in such distress I couldn't even speak. Once they calmed me down and I explained what happened, they took me back into the living room. They practically had to drag me in there. I stayed behind my bigger father, Oskar, hugging his leg.

"There's nothing on the television," said my other father, Tyler. "See."

When I looked, peeking out behind Oskar, I saw that Berry Bunny was no longer there. The television was just static.

Tyler smacked the television set. He looked at Oskar. "Did you forget to pay the cable bill?"

Oskar shrugged at him. "Um…" he grunted in his deep trucker voice. Then he nodded. "Maybe..."

Tyler just shook his head, turned off the television and went to me. He picked me up in his arms.

"It was nothing," he said. "Just your imagination."

He took me into my bedroom.

"Let's play a game of Candyland and get your mind off of it."

When I woke up the next morning, I remembered it clearly. It wasn't actually a dream. It was a memory that had come back to me, something I'd blocked out for many years. But how could it have been real? The cartoon came out of my television set. Cartoons can't do that in real life. It had to have been a dream.

I decided to call my parents and ask them what they thought. If this really did happen to me they would have remembered calming me down. If your child says they saw an arm come out of the television set, that surely would be something you'd remember.

I called my father Tyler, who was always at home. He was a self-employed portraitist and kind of the homemaker of the family.

"Hey Petey," Tyler said when he picked up the phone. "What's up?"

Tyler always called me Petey.

"Hi Dad-T." I always called Tyler Dad-T, which usually turned into Daddy. I called Oskar Dad-O, which usually turned into Daddio.

"How's school?" he asked. He was obviously in the middle of painting, his phone held between his cheek and shoulder.

"It's fine…" I said.

I didn't know how to ask him. I suddenly felt dumb and awkward.

"What's wrong?" Tyler asked.

Dad-T was always good at sensing when something was wrong with me.

"Well, it's kind of stupid…" I said.

"What is?"

"I've been having these crazy dreams."

"Dreams?" Tyler sounded concerned.

"About a Fruit Fun cereal commercial," I said. "Do you ever remember me talking about a Fruit Fun commercial?"

Tyler was silent. He didn't speak a word.

"I have these memories that just came to me," I said. "I completely forgot about them. There's this cartoon rabbit named Berry Bunny. She used to terrify me."

Tyler's tone was severe when he asked, "Are you seeing Fruit Fun commercials again?"

I paused. He knew exactly what I was talking about.

"Umm…" I began, thrown off by his serious tone. Tyler almost always spoke in a soft, friendly voice. This did not sound like him. "I've had these dreams…"

"But have you been seeing them on the television?" he asked.

"No, I'm just dreaming about them," I said. "Why would I see them on the television?"

"The dreams are just the beginning," he said. "Listen carefully. This is very important. Do you have a television in your dorm?"

"Television? You're beginning to scare me."

But Tyler seemed even more frightened than I was. "Yes, a television. You need to stay away from televisions. If you have one in your room get rid of it."

"But it's Dave's television," I said. "I can't get rid of it."

"You have to. Tell him I'll buy him another one."

"What the heck is this all about?" I asked. "What's going on? What does this have to do with my dreams?"

Tyler calmed himself down.

"This happened twice before," he said, in a softer voice. "We thought it was over."

"What was over?" I asked.

"Look, I can't talk to you about this over the phone," he said, his voice still shaking. "I should come up there and visit you. We need to talk about this in person."

"Why? What's this all about?"

"I really think we should wait," Tyler said. "I don't even know how to tell it all to you."

"Well, you've got to tell me something."

"You…" Tyler began. "You had some mental issues when you were young. Very serious issues." He paused, taking a sip of something on the other line, most likely bourbon. "I'm going to call your doctor about this. We'll come up and see you. Just stay away from televisions. That's what triggers it. Stay away from anything that even resembles a television set."

"Okay, fine," I said. "I'll stay away from the television."

"Good," he said. "I'll be there in a couple of days. Don't worry. It'll all be okay." Another swig of bourbon. This time I could hear the glugging sound as he drank.

"I love you, Petey," he said.

"I love you, too."

Then I hung up the phone. A whole new list of questions flooded my head. The commercials weren't dreams, weren't real. They were delusions. Waking nightmares. I really did need a therapist.

I turned on the television.

It was exactly what I was told not to do, but I had to see what would happen. My father made me too curious. If I didn't then it would be all I would think about. Besides, I'm not a kid anymore. I'm not scared of some weird cartoon commercial, especially if it wasn't real. I couldn't get rid of the television anyway. It was Dave's and we were not on good terms at the moment. Moving his television into someone else's dorm room would definitely start a fight, which would end in the television being put back into place anyway. I decided it would be best to just turn it on and get it over with.

The second the television came on, a bloodcurdling scream hit my ears and I fell back. I scooted away on my butt until my back hit the door of the mini fridge. On the television screen, a man in a flannel shirt was being devoured by a giant snake. It was just a movie. I'd forgotten it was Mega Shark vs Giant Snake Week on the SyFy channel. Dave had been watching it on full volume for the past couple of days.

"Motherfucking SyFy bullshit…" I grumbled as I turned down the volume.

There was nothing to worry about. Just a stupid television show. I turned it off and grabbed my towel, then went to the shower room.

My Anthropology class was in a couple hours. I loved Anthropology. Not only was the subject matter pretty interesting, but the instructor really liked me. She thought I was one of her best students. She kept trying to convince me to choose Anthropology as my major. Even though I'm a junior, I have yet to decide my major. I've taken enough classes that I could get a degree in Anthropology by the end of next year. But what the hell would I do with an Anthropolgy degree? I don't want to teach it. I don't even know if I'd want to be an Anthropologist, if that's even a real career. I'm not a fan of traveling. I just like learning about people and cultures.

In the shower, the tile floor was covered in white goo. I couldn't tell if it was shampoo, or conditioner, or if someone jerked off in there because his roommate wouldn't leave the room. It really could be any one of them. I turned on the shower and washed the goo down the drain, just to make sure.

As I showered, I wondered if Dave was going to tell Peri what I said to him. They had Linguistics together. He'd have the perfect opportunity. Kim was in the class, too, so maybe he wouldn't say anything. He wouldn't want her to be suspicious. But telling Peri was just the sort of thing Dave would do. If they had a moment alone, even a minute, he'd tell her. Then Peri would think I'm jealous and violent. I really didn't want that.

My relationship with Peri was perfect when Dave wasn't in the picture. We had a lot of fun together. She liked my sense of humor, liked tearing my clothes off when she was drunk, liked the way I kissed her on the neck. But when he was around, things changed. I was second best, the runner-up. And the only reason she wasn't with him was because he didn't choose her. Not yet, anyway.

As I showered, the thought of it pissed me off more and more. I squished the soap in my hands, turning it into a blob of white paste. If I had any self respect I would just confront Peri myself and if she really liked Dave I would dump her on the spot. At least then I wouldn't feel used.

Walking back to my dorm room, towel wrapped around my waist, I saw two first-year girls giggling at me as I passed them in the hall. They looked my half-naked body up and down. I smiled at them.

I thought perhaps I should leave Peri. There were plenty of girls on campus I could go for. She's not the only one for me. But once I went into my room, sat down on the couch, naked, I thought about how much I really liked Peri. I didn't want anyone else. I wanted her.

As I got dressed for class, there was laughing and cheering noises coming from behind me. It was coming from the television. I didn't think anything of it at first, still thinking about Dave and Peri. But then I remembered I had turned the television off before going to the shower.

"What should we have for breakfast, Milly?" asked a squealing cartoon child.

I froze, dropped my shirts on the ground.

"I don't know, Robby," said a girl's voice. "What would you like?"

I recognized those voices. They were the children from the cereal commercial.

"I want something sweet and delicious."

I turned around and looked at the screen. It was an old cartoon. The same cartoon from my dreams. The children sat around the table, holding spoons, waiting for breakfast.

"I want Fruit Fun cereal!" said the youngest child.

I couldn't believe I was actually seeing it. I closed my eyes. Opened them. The cartoon was still there.

"Yeah, Fruit Fun cereal!" said another cartoon child.

I went for the remote and hit the power button. The television didn't turn off. My father was right. It wasn't a real commercial. But was it a delusion? It seemed so real.

"But we don't have any Fruit Fun cereal..." the oldest child said.

"Aww..." the children groaned in unison. "We haven't had Fruit Fun cereal in forever..."

I wondered if I should go into the hallway, grab the closest person I could find and bring them into the room. Just to see if they could see what I was watching on the television. But I decided against it. I knew what would happen. They would follow me into the room, see the blank television screen, and think I was crazy. That wasn't an embarrassment I could handle. Rumors in the dorm spread like wildfire.

"Where's Berry Bunny?" asked the young girl. "She always has Fruit Fun cereal for us."

Something inside of me twisted and turned. A deep

sense of dread washed over me. I wanted to get out of there. Run away. I wasn't sure why I was so afraid. It was just a cartoon and it wasn't even real. Just a delusion, like Tyler said. But no matter how much I wanted to run, I wouldn't move. I couldn't take my eyes off of the television screen.

"Did somebody call my name?" asked a squeaky voice from off screen.

Then Berry Bunny showed herself. She stepped into the kitchen, holding boxes of Fruit Fun cereal. But it was no longer the Berry Bunny I remembered. She was older. An adult. Her skin was still pink with purple polka dots. She still had long floppy ears. She still had the big cartoon eyes. But her body was fully formed. She had large pink breasts, curved hips, an adult face. Berry Bunny was all grown up.

"Berry Bunny!" the children cried in excitement. "You're back!"

The Bunny rubbed two of the children's shoulders. "That's right. I'm back. And I've missed you all so much."

Her voice was even different. It was still high-pitched and squeaky-sounding like a cartoon character, but slightly deeper and mature.

"Do you have Fruit Fun cereal for us?" the youngest child asked.

She rubbed the child's head. "I'm sorry, I don't. But I'll get some for you very soon."

Then Berry Bunny looked directly at me, through the television screen.

She said, "Isn't that right, Petey?"
Then she licked her lips.

The door burst open and Dave walked in. When I looked back at the television, Berry Bunny was gone.

"What's up, bro?" he said. "Don't you have class?"

I turned on the television with the remote. Then turned it off. The Fruit Fun commercial was gone.

"I'm not going," I told him.

"Want to play Gears of War?" he asked.

"Sure."

Dave was acting like last night never happened. It was normal for him to do something like that. He was the kind of person who was only bothered by something when he wanted to be bothered by it. At that moment, there was nothing in it for him to hold a grudge against me. A day, a week, or a year later he might change his mind, but at that moment we were cool.

"I'm going to kick your ass," he said, turning on his xbox.

We put on player versus player mode, and shot the hell out of each other for a few hours. It was pretty therapeutic. Good for our friendship. We didn't have to fight in real life. We could just kill each other over and over again in the form of a video game. Unfortunately, Dave was better than me at video games and killed me far more often than I killed him. Still, blowing his head off with a shotgun every once in a while was incredibly satisfying.

"I think Kim's pregnant," Dave said.

He just said it casually, in the same way he'd say we were out of ketchup.

"What? She's pregnant?"

Dave shrugged. "I guess so. I don't know. She was acting weird in Linguistics. I heard her telling Peri something about it after class when she didn't think I was listening."

I couldn't play the game very seriously as Dave told me this. He killed me three times in a row.

"What are you going to do?"

He shot me in the face.

"What do you mean what am I going to do? I'm not the one who's pregnant."

"But you knocked her up," I said.

Dave blew snot into a dirty shirt. "Who says it's mine? She probably fucks other guys all the time. You fucked her. It could even be your kid for all I know."

I shook my head. "It's not mine."

"Did you use condoms?" Dave asked.

"No. She never asked me to."

"Well, I did. Every single time."

"I thought she was on the pill."

"I've never seen her take any. She says they make her sick."

"Are you kidding me?" I asked.

"You fucked up."

I didn't believe him. He had to just be fucking

with me. I was only sleeping with Kim for a couple of weeks. He'd been with her a couple months. Even if he wore condoms and I didn't, it made more sense if it were his. If she got pregnant while I was with her she would have known by then.

"You can have her if you want," Dave said. "I think I'm done with her."

"Are you fucking serious?" I asked.

I couldn't believe he'd just dump her like that.

"I don't want a pregnant girl, especially if she got pregnant fucking another guy." He hit me in the back with a chainsaw gun. "Even if she gets an abortion, I don't want to have to deal with that. She'll get all moody and shit. Kim's already a big enough bitch when she's in a good mood. Fuck dealing with her when her chemistry's out of whack."

Dave was such an asshole. I knew what he was doing. He was trying to use this as an excuse to move from Kim to Peri, not giving a shit about what he'd put Kim through by dumping her at a time like this.

But he was kind of a master of screwing over people. He probably had it all planned out. All he had to do was convince everyone that the baby was mine and all the pieces would fall into place. He'd look justified in breaking up with her, because the baby's not his. I would obviously feel bad about everything and help Kim out as much as I could. Then Peri would leave me for knocking up another woman, even though it happened before we met. The fact that I never told her about me and Kim wasn't going to help the situation either.

The only thing working in my favor was that the baby was most likely Dave's. Even if he said he wore a condom, I didn't really believe him. It had to be his.

As we played Gears of War, the screen cut out. It went black. Just for a second. When the picture came back on, it wasn't Gears of War. It was a cartoon. It was a Fruit Fun commercial.

"Oh, Berry Bunny, can't we have Fruit Fun now?" asked the cartoon children.

I was having another delusion. Right in the middle of the video game.

"What the hell happened?" Dave asked.

"Not quite yet," said Berry Bunny.

Dave watched the television with a confused face. "What the hell is this shit?"

It was as though he was talking about the commercial. But that was impossible. The commercial was just a delusion. It was all in my head.

"You can see it, too?" I asked him.

He didn't respond, intrigued by the commercial.

"Soon you'll be able to eat all the Fruit Fun you want," said Berry Bunny.

"Fruit Fun?" Dave asked. "Isn't that the cereal you talked about the other night? I thought you were just fucking with us."

It was true. He could see it. It wasn't a delusion.

Unless even Dave was a part of my imagination, the commercial was real.

"Yeah…" I said.

"Fruit Fun! Fruit Fun! Fruit Fun!" The children chanted.

"Look at the rabbit chick's giant tits," Dave said. "She's pretty fucking hot for a cereal mascot."

Berry Bunny looked at the screen and smiled at us. She said, "Thank you."

But Dave didn't seem to realize she was talking to him. He lost interest and went to the television to switch the input from the cable to the xbox, assuming that there was nothing at all strange about the commercial, even though it came out of nowhere.

"Let's get back to the game," he said.

The second his finger touched the television button, Berry Bunny reached out of the television and grabbed his wrist. He cried out and yanked his arm out of her pink fingers, then kicked the television over, knocking it screen-first onto the floor.

He looked up at me in shock. "What the fuck?"

It's all he said.

With the television on the ground, we could no longer see the screen. There was no sound coming from it. The commercial wasn't playing. Dave stepped around the television like it was some kind of landmine.

"Let's get out of here," he said. "I'm hungry."

Then we left the room. We didn't talk about what had just happened. Dave just changed the subject to which keg party to hit that night. He obviously couldn't accept what had just happened. It was clear he saw and felt the pink bunny hand grab him from the television screen, but he didn't want to believe it. He put it far away from his mind, thinking that if he ignored it then it never happened.

Even though Dave acted like a tough guy, he spooked easily. He believed in ghosts. He believed in aliens. He believed in the supernatural. And all of it scared the shit out of him.

CHAPTER
FOUR

We met up with Kim and Peri a couple hours later and then went to a kegger in the apartment block past the cemetery. Dave had his arm wrapped around Kim's waist, kissing her neck and laughing with her during the party. I couldn't believe he was acting that way with her after what he said to me about planning to break it off with her. He was so two-faced.

Peri was quiet. She didn't say much to me. She didn't want to drink anything even though she paid ten dollars for a cup.

"What's wrong?" I asked her.

"Nothing," she said.

Her eyes were locked on Kim and Dave, as though she wished he was kissing her instead of Kim. Then she ditched me, sneaking upstairs to smoke a bowl with the stoners. I let her go.

My phone vibrated in my pocket. When I took it out, I saw it was a call from my father, Oskar. I fought my way through the crowd of people until I got out of the party. I answered the phone out on the balcony, a few doors down from the smokers.

"Hey, Dad-O," I said.

"Petey?" Oskar asked in his gruff butcher's voice. "Are you okay?"

His tone was serious and filled with concern, even more so than Tyler's.

"I guess…" I didn't want to tell him what had happened since I spoke to my other father. I didn't want to worry them. "What's up?"

"I heard you were having the dreams again," he said.

"Uh, yeah," I said.

Three nearby partiers roared and raised their cups into the air, yelling, "Drink! Drink!"

I moved farther down the balcony to get away from the noise.

"We're coming to see you tonight," he said. "I'm on my way to pick up your father and then we're headed to the airport."

"I thought you'd be coming in a couple of days."

"I'm sorry, but we need to come now. You need to come home. It's too dangerous for you there."

"Dangerous?"

He paused for a moment, having a difficult time finding the words.

"I've never told anyone about this before…" he said.

"Told anyone what?"

"I didn't think anyone would believe me."

"What are you talking about?"

"Do you remember the time I saved you?" he asked.

"Saved me?"

"From the television," he said.

I paused for a moment. I had no idea what he was talking about.

He continued, "When you were nine years old, I left you alone in the living room while I was pulling weeds in the yard. Even though you used to be scared of those cartoons and the doctor told us never to leave you alone by the television, I did it anyway. I didn't think there was anything wrong with it. I thought if you were having delusions then you'd have them no matter where you were."

He paused for a minute to collect himself. He was having a hard time getting out the words. I'd never seen the big guy cry before, but he seemed on the verge of tears. Not necessarily tears of sadness, but tears of distress.

"When I came back inside, I saw you," he continued. "Your legs were dangling out of the television. At first, I thought you were just crawling on top of the set, being a little kid. I even yelled at you to get down. But then I noticed that the front half of your body was missing. It disappeared inside the television set. You were screaming at the top of your lungs, but the sound of your screams didn't come from your body. They came from the television speakers. They echoed across the room through the surround sound."

As he spoke, the memory started to come back to me. I couldn't believe I'd forgotten the experience. While watching television, the Fruit Fun commercial had come on. I went to change the channel so that I wouldn't have to see it when Berry Bunny reached out of the commercial, grabbed me by the arm and pulled me inside.

"I had no idea what was happening or how it was possible," Oskar continued. "I thought I'd lost my mind. The next thing I knew I had you by the legs, trying to pull you out of the television, as some creature on the other side held onto your arms. Eventually, I got you out."

He paused, waiting for my response. But I couldn't say anything.

"I know it sounds crazy," he said. "I had a hard time believing it myself, even though I saw it with my own two eyes. I even punched that little pink goblin thing right in the face after I pulled you out. My hand went through the screen. It was like a hole into another world. I'd never been more terrified in my whole life."

"How did I forget all this?" I asked him.

"I don't know." His voice trembled. "After that, you were practically catatonic for a few days. You hardly ate or said anything. I watched you every second of every day for weeks. You never spoke about what happened. You never mentioned seeing that damned commercial ever again. It was like it all disappeared. You'd forgotten it all. You were back to your old self. I hoped it was over. I hoped you'd never have an experience like that again."

"Well, it happened again," I said.

He was quiet.

"I saw two more of the commercials," I said. "The

thing even grabbed my friend's arm. Its hand came right out of the television."

He was quiet.

"What am I supposed to do?" I asked my father. "What the hell is that commercial anyway?"

He was still quiet.

When I looked down at my phone, I saw that the battery was dead. My father was no longer on the line.

"Shit..." I said, placing the phone in my pocket.

I'd have to call him back after I got back to my dorm room and could get my charger.

I didn't know how long it would take before my fathers got into town, so I decided I might as well keep drinking. The party was likely the safest place I could be. A lot of people. Not a lot of televisions.

But after only another hour, Kim and Peri wanted to leave. Peri said she wasn't feeling well. Kim didn't like the smell of the place.

We all went to Peri's dorm. Dave and I didn't want to go back to ours after what had happened earlier. We didn't mention why. Dave just said the place was a mess. But Peri's dorm didn't allow boys after dark, so we had to sneak in through the side door and keep quiet. Dave didn't really care about getting Peri into trouble, though, and spoke in his loudest voice all the way down the hallway.

"Do you have a phone charger?" I asked Peri when we got into the room.

She handed it to me without saying a word. But the cord wouldn't work. It wasn't the right size for my phone. I hoped I could send Oskar a text to tell him I was alright. Getting cut off like that surely worried him, and they needed to know they could reach me once they got into town, but there wasn't anything I could do at the moment.

"Want to play a drinking game?" Peri asked.

She pulled out a bottle of vodka from behind her bed and a deck of cards from her desk. At the party, she said she wasn't feeling well, acting all tired and sick. But at that moment, she seemed perfectly fine.

"Let's play Asshole," Dave said.

"Fuck that." Peri took off her glasses and let her hair down. "Let's play strip poker."

"Hell yeah!" Dave said. "Let's do it."

I couldn't believe Peri was pulling this shit. The only reason to play strip poker would be because you wanted to see somebody naked that you've never seen naked before. Dave, Kim, and I had already seen each other naked several times in the past. The only people who hadn't seen each other without clothes were Peri and Dave, which meant they both wanted to see each other naked. I wondered if Peri knew Dave was going to break up with Kim. I wondered if she planned to make a move on him, or at least get him interested in her if he saw her naked, convince him to make a move on her.

54

"I don't want to play strip poker," Kim said.

"Yeah, let's just play Asshole," I said. "Or Kings or something."

But Peri and Dave were adamant about it.

"You fucking pussies," Peri said. "Come on. Let's play."

"Yeah, what are you embarrassed of your bodies?" Dave said. "I'm the fattest one here and you don't see me complaining."

Peri looked at Dave in shock, eying his body up and down, and said, "You're not fat!"

"You haven't seen me naked…" Dave told her.

"Not yet!" she said with excitement. Then she giggled.

Their flirtatious routine was getting under my skin. They were flirting with each other right in front of Kim and I, not even trying to hide it. If they were drunk it might have been more understandable, even somewhat forgivable, but Peri didn't even have a sip of alcohol.

I looked at Kim, but she didn't seem to know or even care about their behavior. I had a feeling she was losing interest in Dave even more than he was losing interest in her.

"So are you in or out?" Dave asked us.

"Fine," Kim said with a groan. "Whatever."

I agreed as well. I knew they would just play without me if I refused and it was better to be in than out.

When we anteed up for the first hand, we each threw in an article of clothing into the pot. Everyone threw in one shoe except for Peri who took her top off and tossed it into the pile.

Only Dave cried out in excitement as she removed her shirt, revealing a newly purchased purple lace bra.

"Damn, girl!" Dave cried. "You know how to party!"

That's when I knew I was fucked. Peri wasn't mine anymore. She wanted Dave and was going after him with everything she had. Kim just rolled her eyes at Peri's act, dismissing her as a dork or a slut. She obviously didn't give a shit or feel threatened by the girl. Or maybe she had bigger problems to worry about now that she knew she was pregnant, especially if it wasn't Dave's kid.

Peri didn't look at me as we played cards, blocking me out, pretending I wasn't even there. She only spoke to Dave. It was incredibly irritating. I wanted to just get up and walk out of there, leave them without saying a word. It didn't really matter either way. My fathers were coming to pick me up soon anyway. They said they were going to take me home. With me out of the picture, Dave and Peri would have all the opportunity they needed to get together.

"Three aces!" Dave cried when we showed our hands.

He had the winning hand and got the pot of clothes. When he picked up my girlfriend's shirt, he brought it to his face and deeply inhaled her fragrance.

"Mmmm…" he said, letting out a long sigh.

Peri just giggled at him.

"What the fuck?" I said, as Dave continued smelling my girlfriend's shirt.

Dave and Peri glanced at me with annoyed expressions. Dave dropped the shirt as though I'd spoiled all his fun.

"I'm sick of this bullshit," I said.

Dave acted innocent. "Relax, bro. I'm just joking around."

"Yeah, stop being a dick," Peri said.

"*I'm* being a dick?" I asked.

My face was burning red. I could feel the heat rising in my cheeks. I wanted to knock Dave out for pulling this shit in front of me.

"Chill out," Dave said.

"Fuck this," I said, tossing my cards onto the floor. "I'm out of here."

Dave stood up and blocked my path to the door. For some reason, he didn't want me to leave.

"Come on, bro. It's nothing. Honest." He handed me the bottle of vodka. "Have a drink. Loosen up."

Peri didn't say anything. She probably wanted me to go.

I took the bottle, poured a long shot down my throat, and sat back down. I didn't really want to leave anyway. The thought of going back to my dorm alone didn't sound like a good idea. So I sat there and continued to play the game. Dave behaved himself after that. For the moment, at least.

The television turned itself on while we were playing cards. We all stopped what we were doing, jumping from our seats like a ghost had walked through the room. Both of the girls let out quick screams and then laughed when they realized it was just the television.

Dave and I weren't laughing. When we saw the Fruit Fun commercial on the screen, both of us looked at each other with wide open eyes. Dave looked like he was about to shit his pants, inching slowly away from the screen.

"What's this?" Kim asked.

Berry Bunny was hopping up and down on the screen. "Are you ready for a nutritious breakfast?"

The children cried, "Fruit Fun! Fruit Fun!"

Peri was annoyed that the television interrupted their game of strip poker. She grabbed the remote and pushed the power button. The television didn't turn off.

"The batteries are dead…" she said, tossing the remote.

She got to her feet.

"What's going on with that cartoon?" Kim asked.

The way Kim looked at the television, she seemed to know something was wrong with it. Even though she didn't experience what Dave and I had, she seemed just as anxious about it.

Only Peri was oblivious to the danger. She went toward the television set to turn it off.

"Don't!" I cried.

But there was nothing I could do. She went straight up to the television. Dave was close enough to stop her, but he didn't move. He wouldn't go near it. Didn't care what happened to her as long as it wasn't him.

"Just a little closer," said Berry Bunny.

Dave and I saw the rabbit's eyes locked on Peri as she approached. Then the cartoon leapt out of the screen.

"What the fuck!" Peri cried, her voice a shriek.

The rabbit grabbed her by the arm with one hand, then seized her bra with the other. Peri kept screaming, trying to latch onto something to keep herself in the room.

"Do something!" Kim cried, kicking Dave.

But Dave wouldn't move. He was frozen in place.

The bunny tugged Peri into the screen, hitting her head against the edge of the television. Peri's body went limp, no longer fighting it.

I ran across the room, reaching for her legs. But before I could grab them, she was all the way inside the commercial.

"What the hell just happened?" Kim cried.

I couldn't believe it. Inside the commercial, Peri was being dragged across the kitchen floor by Berry Bunny. Only it didn't look like Peri anymore. She was a cartoon. It was her, though. The limp cartoon character was wearing her jeans, her purple bra, had her dirty blond hair.

"They took her…" I said.

Kim got to her feet, rushing toward me. "What do we do? What the fuck do we do?"

The cartoon Peri regained consciousness. She looked around the kitchen, looked at the bunny pulling at her arms.

"Help me!" she screamed, yelling at us through the television screen. "Oh, God, help me…"

She kicked at the bunny until she was able to break free. Berry Bunny blocked her path back toward us, so Peri ran in the opposite direction. She left the cartoon kitchen, running off screen, the bunny chasing after. We could still hear her screams as she ran deeper and deeper into the commercial.

We all stood there, staring at each other, not sure what to do. The commercial didn't stop. It just went on, even though there weren't any characters on the screen. The cartoon children were nearby. We could hear them kicking their legs and playing with their spoons. But they didn't speak. They didn't say anything.

"What the hell is going on…" Kim said. "What do we do?"

I looked at them. "We have to go in and save her."

"Fuck that," Dave said. "I'm not going in there."

"We have to save her," I said.

Dave shook his head. "Fuck her. She's *your* girlfriend. *You* save her."

"Fine, I'll go alone," I said.

Kim grabbed my arm. "You can't go in there."

I looked at the cartoon and put my hand inside, just for a second. It didn't feel any different. Just like sticking my hand through a window. It was surreal seeing the cartoon version of my hand on the other side of the screen. There were no details in the skin. Just a smooth peach-colored hand-shaped blob.

When I pulled my hand out, I looked at Kim and said, "I have to."

I couldn't leave Peri in the commercial. I knew what would happen to her if I left her in there. And even though Peri didn't want me, even if she'd rather be with Dave, I still loved her. I couldn't handle the thought of anything happening to her.

Dave stood behind me, peering into the screen from behind my shoulder.

"Good luck, bro," he said.

I couldn't tell if he was being genuine or telling me I was fucked if I stepped foot inside of there.

"I'll need it," I said.

But before I could climb into the cartoon world, the television moved. I stepped back. The screen grew. It expanded, opening like a garage door on all four sides.

"What's happening?" Kim asked.

We all backed away.

The screen stretched all the way up to the ceiling, all the way down to the floor. The sides widened across the walls, swallowing Peri's shelves and desk. When it was finished, the television screen was as large as the entire south side of the room. It was big enough that we could all just walk right into the cartoon kitchen. We could even drive a truck in there.

"We need to get out of here," Dave said.

But before we could go for the door, the cartoon

stretched even further. It moved toward us, swallowing the dorm room, covering the door and window, blocking our only escape.

We backed up as the room became a part of the commercial. The shoes we had taken off, Peri's shirt, the cards, the bottle of vodka—it all became cartoon as the screen moved forward.

Dave and Kim screamed. They held each other, backed up in the corner of the room, into Peri's closet. I looked at the back wall, wondering if we could break it down in time to escape. But the wall was brick and the television screen was moving too fast.

We just looked at each other in shock as the cartoon swallowed us whole and we were sucked into the television set.

CHAPTER
FIVE

Inside the commercial, we weren't turned into cartoons as Peri had been. On this side of the screen, nothing was cartoon. Everything was brightly colored and proportioned the same way as the cartoon had been, but it was all real. It was three-dimensional. On the other side of the screen, we most likely did appear to be cartoons if anyone happened to have been watching us. But inside the television, the world was as real as the world out there.

Kim was hysterical. She clawed at the wall which was once dorm room, trying to break through to the other side.

"What the hell is this?" she cried. "How do we get out of here?"

But no matter how hard she tried, she couldn't even put a scratch on the bright yellow kitchen wallpaper.

Behind us, the children sat at the breakfast table. They just sat there, eyeballing each other with their eyes spread too far apart on their faces. The sight of the deformed cartoons-made-flesh made my skin curl and shiver. I wouldn't go near them.

"Is it time for Fruit Fun, Milly?" asked the youngest boy. His voice was distorted and strange in their world. It made sense as a cartoon, but was now shrill and horrific.

The oldest girl said, "Almost, Robby. Almost."

They didn't acknowledge us in the room. It didn't seem like they knew we were there.

"What the fuck are they?" Dave asked me, yelling at me in the loudest whisper possible. His face was distressed.

"The cartoon kids," I said.

"They're not fucking cartoons," Dave whisper-cried.

I just shook my head. "I know they're not."

Kim went to me. "How do we get out of here? What's going to happen to us?"

I didn't know how to get out. The television screen was the only way through, but the television screen was nowhere to be seen. We were trapped.

"Let's go find Peri," I said to them.

They looked at me in a panic. They didn't want to leave the kitchen. If that was the room they entered into then it was more likely to be the room they could escape.

"She's probably dead, bro," Dave said. "Forget about her."

I went toward the kitchen exit. "Stay here if you want. I'm going after her."

The second I stepped out of the kitchen, the other two followed me.

The hallway leading to the front door was less decorated than the kitchen. The walls were yellow, but less bright, just pale in color. The lights were dim.

"You think she went outside?" Dave asked.

I nodded. "She might have gone upstairs, but I doubt it. The front door is open."

It was only open a crack, but it made sense she would have come this way. If I were her I would have ran for the door. Going upstairs would have been a death trap.

I opened the door and looked outside.

"What's out there?" Dave asked.

"A neighborhood," I said. "Sort of…"

We stepped through the doorway and looked around. It was quiet and empty, like an abandoned movie set. The houses and cars parked on the street were brightly colored. They were clean and glistening. It was obvious nobody was living in these homes. Nobody had ever lived in them.

"Let's go," I said.

I walked into the street, looking down the road, wondering which direction she might have gone. There was no sound coming from anywhere in the neighborhood. No screams for help. Not even wind. Just silence. Like we were inside a vacuum.

"We should split up," I told them.

Dave shook his head. "We're not splitting up."

"But there's two directions she could have gone.

If we go the wrong way it might be too late."

"It's probably already too late," Dave said.

We decided to go to the right. The road curved in that direction. It looked more inviting to somebody who was trying to escape.

"This way," I said.

They followed me down the road, scanning the houses for Peri. The ground felt strange beneath our feet. It wasn't rough asphalt. It was smooth like ceramic tile, colored dark gray.

We tried to go into one of the houses, but the door wasn't real. It was just painted onto the wall. We looked inside the window. It was empty inside. No furniture. No doors. Just a large empty room.

"She wouldn't have gone into any of these," Kim said as she peered into a window.

The farther away from the original house we got, the darker everything became. Even though the morning sun was in the unmoving blue sky, it was not bright enough to provide light for the whole neighborhood. The colors became duller. Everything lacked detail. It was like we were walking into the background of a painting. Only the foreground was painted intricately. Everything else faded into shapeless blurs the farther we went.

"I don't want to keep going this way," Kim said.

We were all in agreement. After just a few blocks, the neighborhood started to disappear. Everything was dark, colorless. The houses were just outlines with no windows or doors. The sky was a blank piece of paper.

It was like we were stepping through a line drawing.
And beyond the lines there was only darkness. The
gray melted to black. There was only nothingness.

But within the nothingness, within the dark, there
was movement. I could hear things crawling and
breathing in the black, shapeless creatures waiting
for us to enter. I couldn't tell if there was only one
large creature or hundreds of them, but they sounded
wild and ferocious, like demonic dragons, like black
beast-like balls of claws and teeth. When the others
heard the growling and shuffling, they froze in their
place, terrified of whatever it was that hid inside of
the black. We instantly turned around, back toward
the neighborhood, back toward the main section of
the commercial.

The cartoon world was not large. It was small.
Very small. It wasn't going to be easy to hide from
Berry Bunny in such a place. I hoped Peri was alright.

We searched the neighborhood for what felt like hours.
The more we searched, the smaller the neighborhood
felt and the larger the surrounding darkness became.

"I don't like it out here," Kim said, sitting on the
curb and rubbing her shoeless foot.

"Yeah," Dave said. "We should go back to the main
house."

I shook my head. "She's got to be here somewhere."

As we continued the search, I didn't leave any stone unturned. I looked inside every car, every house window. Everything was hollow inside. Like a prop or a toy. The wheels of the cars didn't even turn, embedded in the street.

In the distance, we saw something moving. It wasn't Peri. It was pink and purple and hopped down the road. Berry Bunny was on the hunt.

The second we saw her, we got off the road. We ran between the two nearest houses and hid in a backyard, behind a group of fake trees. Then we waited.

As Berry Bunny hopped past, we watched through plastic leaves.

"Come out, children," the bunny said. "You have to try my Fruit Fun cereal. It's delicious and good for you, too!"

She looked into the yard we were in, but didn't look closely enough. She just took one glance and hopped on, staying on the main road.

"Are you out there?" she asked. "Aren't you hungry?"

The sight of her in human form sent shivers down my spine. She wasn't a cartoon anymore. She was like a normal woman wearing a cheap bunny costume. Her skin was like she was naked with pink and purple body paint. Her large feet, fluffy tail, twitching whiskers and long floppy ears were like rubber prosthetics. The only thing that proved she wasn't just a woman in a costume was her large round eyes that bulged out of her head like a creepy Blythe doll.

She said, "Come on, Petey. I've been waiting for

you for so long. All you need to do is take one bite and you'll be hooked for life."

The bunny beckoned us to come out of hiding, but we knew that would be a fatal mistake. We didn't move an inch. We didn't even breathe.

None of us said a word until the bunny was long gone.

"What are we going to do?" Kim cried, still shaking from the sight of the monstrous rabbit woman.

I didn't have an answer for her. But one thing I did know, Berry Bunny didn't have Peri yet. If she did she wouldn't be hunting. Wherever Peri was, she was safe, for now. That is, as long as she didn't go into the blackness surrounding the neighborhood.

"That thing called your name," Dave said to me. "She said *Petey*. How did she know your name?"

I shook my head, tried to play ignorant. "How should I know? She's a fucking cereal mascot that eats children."

But the second I said that, I knew they wouldn't buy it. I had already revealed more than I was letting on.

"Wait a minute…" Dave said. "What do you mean she eats children?"

I couldn't hide it any longer. I told them everything. About my childhood. About the commercials. About being pulled into the television and saved by my father. About the tiny children that were eaten like cereal.

"Are you fucking kidding me?" Dave asked, pissed off at me for not telling them sooner. "You knew all of this the whole time?"

Kim paced back and forth in the fake velvety grass. "Is that what she wants? She's going to eat us?"

I shook my head. "I don't know. I think so."

"What do you mean you *think* so?" Kim cried.

"She was eating shrunken children in the commercial, so it is possible she plans to shrink us and eat us. But I don't know. Maybe that wasn't real. Maybe it was just designed to scare me."

But Kim was convinced that it was going to happen. "I don't want to be eaten like cereal! We have to get out of here!"

Dave grabbed me by the shirt and pushed me to the ground. "This is your fault, you motherfucker. *You* did this."

"How did *I* do this?" I asked.

Before I could get up, he pushed me back down.

"That bunny was after you. Ever since you were a kid, she was after you. Not us. If it wasn't for you none of this would have happened."

"It would have happened to me," I said.

"Yeah, but *just* you," he said. "The rest of us would be safe."

"But what about me?" I asked. "You don't give a shit if it happened to me?"

Dave spit on the ground. "Better just you than all of us."

I stood up and Dave got into my face, ready to

unleash all of his anger and aggression on me. He probably would have decked me if Kim didn't get between us.

She pushed Dave back. "Stop it. That thing is going to hear you."

When Dave calmed down, she said, "We need to figure a way out of here."

I agreed. "But first we have to find Peri. She's still out there somewhere."

We eventually found Peri on the back porch of one of the mock houses on the outskirts of the neighborhood, one of the dark colorless houses.

She was curled up in a ball, shivering, mumbling nonsense to herself.

"Is she okay?" Kim asked.

She was in such a frantic state that she scared us. We thought she was some kind of creature lurking in the dark, going to leap out and attack at any second.

The others stayed back as I approached her.

"Peri?" I asked. "Per—"

She didn't look up at me. She didn't speak. It was like she didn't even know I was there. Cuts and bruises were all over her legs and arms. She must have fallen down several times trying to escape the bunny woman.

"Come on," I said to her, lifting her to her feet. "We need to go."

She was able to walk on her own, even though her mind was miles away. It was like all the times I had to escort her back to her dorm room whenever she got blackout drunk. But this time it was life or death.

"Let's go back to the house," I told the others.

They followed after me, watching the streets for any signs of the cartoon rabbit.

For days, we tried to find ways out of the commercial. We searched the house for signs of an exit, signs of a television screen. But there was none to be found. The only one who would have the answer was Berry Bunny, but we knew to stay far away from her.

Kim tried asking the children. She went up to them, slammed her fist on the table.

"How do we get out?" she cried.

But the children didn't acknowledge her. They just looked at each other with beady eyes, tilting their bulbous heads, and every once in a while smacking the table with their large metal spoons. They were like creepy cabbage patch kids the size of adults, but they drooled and breathed and smelled like old ham.

"Talk to me, you little shits," she said.

She smacked one of them on the back of the head, but it still didn't acknowledge her.

"I wouldn't do that if I were you," Dave said, too terrified to get anywhere near the kids.

"Fuck them," she said. She smacked the kid again. "I'll hit them as many times as it takes until they tell us how to get out of here."

She smacked each of them as hard as she could. Then she tossed their bowls from the table, smashed them on the floor. They still didn't look at her or move from their spots, just drooling and staring like malformed cartoon zombies.

We spent our days in the kitchen of the house. It was the brightest place in the cartoon and felt the safest, even with the horrifying children at the breakfast table. That was where the commercial took place. If the gateway to our world ever opened it would happen there, so that was where we spent most of our time.

Sometimes we took shifts sleeping in the kitchen or on the hard plastic couch-shaped blocks in the living room, but we mostly slept in the upstairs bedrooms. There were no beds or furniture up there, just empty rooms with no windows. But the doors locked. They felt safe. And nothing ever tried to come inside with us. The only problem was how uncomfortable it was trying to sleep on the hard carpet-colored ceramic tile flooring.

Outside of the house became more frightening with each passing day. We heard the noises of the shuffling creatures out there, coming closer and closer all the time. The darkness seemed to squeeze in around the house. Nobody wanted to go out there for any reason. We'd already explored the area out there so many times there didn't really seem to be a need to investigate it further.

Berry Bunny rarely came into the house. Whenever she did, she just came to visit the children. She gave them bowls of pink cereal. It wasn't miniature people. It was actual cereal now. The children ate it up with glee.

During her visits, we always hid in the cabinets and behind the curtains. She never looked for us in these places. It was like she forgot we were even in their world. She never spoke about us or called out to us as she did the first day. We made sure not to make a single sound or breathe a single breath while she was in the house. If just one of us were found she'd surely get us all.

For food, we ate Fruit Fun cereal. There were multiple boxes in the cupboard near the refrigerator. And there was milk in a glass pitcher on the breakfast table that never got warm and always seemed to replenish itself whenever we weren't looking.

Fruit Fun cereal seemed like any old cereal. It had the shape and texture of Trix or Cocoa Puffs, only the small round balls were pink and tasted like artificial strawberry. The best part about it was that it turned the milk pink and made it taste a bit like Strawberry Quik. But the stuff was really sweet and after a couple of days of eating nothing else it was making us all sick.

If we ever get out of this commercial, I'll never eat another bowl of cereal for the rest of my life.

CHAPTER
SIX

We are hiding from Berry Bunny again. Kim and Dave are in the cabinets. Peri is in the refrigerator. I'm behind the curtains, watching through the loosely-stitched fabric. Berry Bunny shows off her brightly colored boxes of Fruit Fun, then fills the children's bowls to the brim with the pink balls of cereal. After all their bowls are full, she pours the milk and the children dig in.

"Thank you, Berry Bunny!" the children cry. "You're the best!"

Berry Bunny smiles with pride. "And don't forget that it's not only delicious. It contains over thirteen vitamins and minerals, so it's the perfect way to start the day!"

Three of the children eat the cereal with laughter and merriment, savoring every bite. But one of them doesn't touch it. The youngest child just stares at the bowl with a frown on his face.

"What's wrong, Robby?" Berry Bunny asks the boy. "Don't you like your Fruit Fun?"

Robby shakes his head.

"This isn't *real* Fruit Fun," he says.

He pushes the bowl away.

"Whatever do you mean, Robby?" asks Berry Bunny.

"I want the tasty kind," he says. "The kind that wiggles and squirms. It's not *real* Fruit Fun unless it makes my belly feel like it's dancing with happiness."

The other children look at each other and frown. They all push their bowls away as well.

"Yeah, this kind just isn't the same," says Milly.

Berry Bunny smacks her palm to her pink face and makes an exaggerated O-shape with her mouth.

"Well, this just won't do," says Berry Bunny. "If this cereal isn't good enough then you'll just have to get some new and improved Fruit Fun."

The children cry, "New and improved! New and improved!"

Berry Bunny steps away from the table toward the kitchen area. "Let me just see what we have in the cupboards."

"New and improved! New and improved!"

As Berry Bunny opens the cabinet doors one after another, my pulse quickens, my breath becomes heavy. She's going to find my friends and there's nothing I can do to prevent it. I wonder if I should leave my hiding spot and create a distraction. I wonder if I should run for it, try to lead her outside, away from the others.

"What kind of Fruit Fun would you like?" asks Berry Bunny. "Boy or girl?"

"Girl!" the children cry. "Girl! Girl!"

Berry Bunny nods at them. "Girl it is."

The rabbit woman opens the cabinet Kim's hiding in and grabs her by the legs.

"Get off me!" Kim cries.

She kicks at Berry Bunny, hitting her in the breasts and belly, but it doesn't stop the rabbit from pulling her out onto the kitchen floor. Kim's either too weak from malnutrition and stress or the bunny is too strong. Either way, she can do nothing to keep the bunny off of her.

I hesitate for a second. A part of me wants to keep out of danger and save myself, another part of me expects Dave to try to save his girlfriend. If Dave does try to help her I'll back him up without a second thought. But Dave does nothing. He stays hidden.

The children pound their spoons on the table, "Girl! Girl! Girl! Girl!"

Kim cries, "Don't touch me, you freak! Get off me!"

I realize it's up to me to save her. Dave, the selfish asshole, isn't going to do a thing, even for his pregnant girlfriend.

"Leave her alone," I yell, running out from behind the curtain.

But I can't reach her in time. Berry Bunny pulls Kim to her feet and grips her by the waist, pulling her close to her bosom. Kim punches and screams as a warm glow envelops her. Some kind of pink energy issues from the bunny's palms, digging into Kim's flesh, transforming her. Kim's screams become splintered into thousands.

I grab Berry Bunny's rubbery arm just as the process

is complete. Kim's skin splits and cracks, then she shatters into a thousand pieces.

"Girl! Girl! Girl! Girl!"

At first, I think Kim is melting into a puddle on the floor. A pink blob oozes out of her clothes, slipping out of her shirt sleeves, pouring out of her pant legs. But she's not melting. She's become fragmented. On the kitchen floor, I see hundreds of miniature copies of Kim. All of them pink and naked. All of them the same size as the pink balls of Fruit Fun cereal.

Berry Bunny turns and eyeballs me, licking her whiskers.

"Breakfast is ready," she says to me.

"Yay!" the children cry, throwing their chubby arms up in triumph.

I don't move, worried about where to step. I'm standing ankle-deep inside of a large puddle of screaming Kims. I can hear her tiny distant voices crying and begging for help.

Berry Bunny scoops the miniature Kims up into empty cereal boxes. I don't try to stop her, worried that if she touches me I'll end up another puddle of tiny people on the floor.

"Fruit Fun! Fruit Fun!" the children cry.

As Berry Bunny pours a box of Kims into their cereal bowls, Dave takes the opportunity to make a break for it. He jumps out of the cabinet and runs through the puddle of Kims, squashing dozens of her beneath his feet. He knocks me out of the way as he races for the front door, but I hold my balance, not wanting to carelessly crush the shrunken Kims in the same way Dave did.

"Where you going?" I yell at him.

But he doesn't say a thing. He probably doesn't even hear me, just charging forward at full speed, trying to get as far away as humanly possible. And after he's gone, Peri jumps out of the refrigerator. She slides in the puddle of Kims, smearing their bodies against the tile floor and lands butt-first right in the middle of it. When she gets up and rushes past me, I can see a large smudge of Kim paste covering the right cheek of her jeans.

I stay behind, not sure what to do. I want to save Kim, but in her current state I'm not sure how.

Berry Bunny pours milk over the bowls full of Kim on the breakfast table. Then the children dig in. They scoop spoonfuls of the screaming naked girl into their globular gaping mouths and swallow them with delighted gulps.

"This is delicious!" one child cries.

"Thank you, Berry Bunny!" says another. "You're the best!"

The sight of my friend being eaten by the horrific children fills me with rage. As the bunny is busy scooping up the rest of the Kims into cereal boxes, I rush the breakfast table.

"Stop it!" I cry.

I try to grab a bowl from one of the children. I tighten my grip around his bowl with one hand and seize his wrist with the other, holding back the spoon of Kims just inches from his gaping lips.

"Let go, you ugly fuck…" I cry.

The child is strong. Much stronger than he looks. I can't pull the bowl or spoon away from him.

"Mine!" the child cries.

Then he smacks me with his free arm and I find myself airborne, flying across the kitchen and crashing into the refrigerator. My body leaves a large dent in its side.

Before I can get to my feet, Berry Bunny stands over me, holding a bowl full of naked Kims.

"Have a bite, Petey," she says to me. "You'll just love my delicious cereal. I promise you will."

She scoops up a spoonful of Kims and holds it up to my face.

"Pete!" the Kims cry, staring me in the eyes as they swim in the pink milk. "Help me! They're eating me!"

I push the spoon away and run. I don't know what else to do. The thought of leaving her crushes the heart in my chest. I loved her once, before she left me for Dave. I care for her even still. But there's nothing I can do to save her. Even if I grabbed a handful of her before I ran, I'd never be able to put her together again. She's already dead.

Berry Bunny follows after me as I run out of the house and into the fake morning sunlight. She carries her bowl of cereal, eating spoonfuls of Kim as she moves toward me.

I run down the street until I catch up to Peri. She's standing in the middle of the road, deep in the shapeless gray area of the world, a panicked look painted across her face.

"Help him!" Peri cries.

She's no longer catatonic, finally snapped back into consciousness. She comes to me and grabs at my clothes.

"He's in there," she says. "You have to do something."

Then I hear it. Dave's voice. He ran all the way into the blackness at the edge of the world.

"He went in there?" I ask, pointing at the blank nothingness.

She nods at me.

Dave's cries echo through the black, coming at us from a hundred directions, followed by the sound of a hundred ferocious animals ripping apart their prey.

"Get him out," Peri cries, tears flowing down her cheeks. "You have to get him out of there."

But before I have to make the choice, Dave is thrown out of the black and lands in the street. We run toward him.

"Dave!" Peri cries. "Are you alright?"

She runs to him, falls to her knees and holds him

in her arms, pressing her purple bra against his cheek. I wonder if she'd react the same way if I was the one who was injured.

"Dave?" I ask, not sure if he's alive or dead.

When I see him, I can't believe his state. He's been torn up by some kind of creature. His clothes are ripped open, revealing deep bloody gashes on his chest and stomach. Large chunks of flesh are missing from his face and arms.

"He's dying," Peri says. "You have to do something."

But there's nothing I can do. He's too torn up. His right leg is missing most of its flesh. He's bleeding out and will be dead within minutes.

"The commercial…" Dave says, choking on his own blood.

"What?" Peri asks him. Then she looks at me. "What's he saying?"

We listen more carefully.

He says, "It's not for us…" Then he points at the blackness. "It's for them…"

Peri asks, "What's for them? What do you mean?"

His eyes glaze over. Peri shakes him, trying to wake him up.

I look back and see Berry Bunny closing in on us.

"Come on," I say, grabbing Peri by the arm. "We have to go."

Peri resists. "We can't leave him!"

I shake my head and pull her away with all my strength. "There's nothing we can do."

When Peri sees the bunny coming at us, she stops resisting. She leaves my arms and runs toward the backs of the houses. I follow her.

The bunny doesn't come for us. She goes to Dave's body. He wiggles and twitches as she stands over him, still a bit of life left in him.

From a safe distance, we watch. Peri holds me from behind.

"Is she going to turn him into cereal?" Peri asks.

Berry Bunny leans down to Dave. She scoops out a spoonful of Kims and lowers it to his face.

"Have some Fruit Fun cereal," the bunny says. "It'll pick you right up!"

Then she puts the spoon in his mouth.

"No…" I say. "She's feeding him."

As Dave swallows, something changes in him. His wounds heal. He gets up to his feet and stares the bunny in the eyes.

"Is he alright?" Peri asks, relief in her voice. "Is he going to live?"

Dave goes to Berry Bunny and yanks the bowl out of her hand. She gives him the spoon. Like a starving madman, he proceeds to devour the bowl of shrunken Kims, shoveling bite after bite into his mouth as fast as he can.

We can't hear the miniature Kims from this distance, but they're surely screaming in terror as they are eaten by the man who was once her boyfriend.

"There, there," Berry Bunny says to Dave, stroking the back of his head like a cat. "Eat all you want. It's always a fun time with Fruit Fun."

Peri covers her mouth and screams through her fingers. She notices it before I do. As Dave is eating, his body transforms. His cheeks widen. His belly grows fat. His eyes shrink and widen on his face. By the time he's finished and drinks the leftover milk in the bowl, the transformation is complete. He has become one of the cartoon children.

"Isn't it delicious?" Berry Bunny asks him. "Everyone loves my Fruit Fun cereal. It's an important part of a balanced breakfast."

As Berry Bunny leads the plump malformed version of Dave up the street, back toward the breakfast table, we hide in the bushes and wait for them to pass. That thing isn't Dave anymore. Whatever it is, he's one of them now.

CHAPTER
SEVEN

We spend hours hiding out in the yard. Berry Bunny doesn't come back, but we still don't want to leave our hiding spot. Peri has her arms wrapped around me, holding me tightly to her, resting her face in my chest with her eyes closed tight. It feels good to be holding her again. I still love her. Even though she probably would have preferred I was the one who was transformed into a hideous cereal-eating monster back there instead of Dave, even though she surely planned to leave me for him the first moment she got, it still feels good to be within her embrace once again. If I die, at least I'll die having spent one last moment of tenderness with her.

"I love you," she tells me.

I can't tell how sincere she is by saying that. Part of me thinks she's only saying this now that Dave is gone. Part of me thinks she just wants me to believe she loves me so that I'll stand by her, protect her with my life. I'm all she has now.

"You know that, right?" she asks.

I nod, even though I don't believe a word of it. "I love you, too."

She squeezes me. "I'm sorry for being a bitch."

"You're not a bitch," I say.

"Yeah, I am."

"Don't worry about it," I tell her, weaving my fingers through her hair. "I would have understood if you left me. Especially after what happened with Kim."

Peri tenses up for a moment. She looks up at me with a confused expression. "What happened with Kim?"

"You know…" I say. "Her getting pregnant."

Her face tenses. "Who told you that?"

"Dave," I say. "He said he overheard her talking to you about it after Linguistics class. He said it was likely mine."

Peri shakes her head. "Kim's not pregnant."

"What?"

Peri sits up. "It's not Kim we were talking about." She presses her hand to her stomach. "It was me."

"You're…"

She nods. "I'm the one who's pregnant."

I sit up with a jerk. "What! You're pregnant? Why didn't you tell me?"

She breaks eye contact. "I wasn't going to…"

"Why not?" I ask.

She doesn't speak for a moment, not sure how to explain.

"Because…" she says. "Because I was going to have an abortion."

I squeeze her hand. "You still should have told

me. If you planned to have an abortion I would have been there for you. I wouldn't want you to go through that alone."

She shakes her head and pulls her hand away. "You don't understand."

"What don't I understand?"

She looks me in the eyes. "If I told you then I would have decided against having an abortion. I would want to have the child. I would want to marry you."

"So what's wrong with that?"

"I'm only twenty," she says. "I'm not ready to get married or have a kid. I want to have a career. That's why I couldn't tell you. If you were interested in the idea I would have made that choice without hesitation."

I stay silent, not sure what to say.

"Look, you're the perfect guy," she says. "You're exactly the kind of guy I see myself marrying in eight to ten years, when I'm ready. You're nice, supportive, fun to be around. You'd probably make a great father. But I'm not ready for that. I'm still in college. I should be dating dumb guys that don't mean anything to me. Guys who are fun to be around but aren't worth getting serious with. Guys like Dave."

I look at my hands when she mentions Dave. She really was trying to leave me for him.

She says, "I wanted to fuck up our relationship on purpose so that it would have been easier for me to make the decision. I'm sorry, but I'm just not ready to be a mother."

"What about your parents?" I ask. "I thought they

were religious and totally against abortion."

She shrugs. "I wasn't planning on telling them either. Same reason."

I don't say anything more. I let it go. After all we'd been through, I didn't want to fault her for her choices. I didn't want to judge her for them. I just wanted to hold her. Be with her.

"If we get out of this, you'll marry me won't you?" she asks me. "If I decide to have the baby you'll have it with me, right?"

I pause for a moment. I want her words to be true, but there's something in the tone of her voice, something insincere. It's the same tone she takes whenever she's lying to me. I don't think she really means anything she's saying. I think she just wants me to believe it, to give me motivation to keep her alive.

"I'd like to," I say. "But ask me again. Once we get out of here." I squeeze her tightly. "This isn't the time to make that kind of decision."

She kisses my chest through my shirt and cuddles into my arm. I stroke her back, closing my eyes, imagining what my life would be like if I actually did marry her. But before the vision can bring a smile to my face, the palm of my hand rubs against a collection of crushed Kim parts glued to the back of Peri's clothes. They get stuck between my fingers, underneath my fingernails.

Peri falls asleep and snores against my chest as I wipe off the bite-sized bits of gore onto the back of her pants.

I let Peri take a long rest against me, but I don't sleep a wink. I don't want to be caught off guard if the bunny comes back for us. As she wakes against my chest, drool soaking my shirt, eyes squinting at the fake morning sun, she looks up and smiles at me with a sad yet contented smile.

"Do you think we'll actually be able to get out of here?" she asks me.

I take a deep breath. "There's only one way."

"What's that?"

"The bunny has to broadcast another commercial," I say. "I believe every time a Fruit Fun commercial appears on a child's television, it opens a gateway between this world and the child's living room. We should be able to get out that way."

"But what if she tries to stop us?"

"Then I'll distract her so you can get through." I kiss the side of her forehead. "Hopefully it won't come to that."

Peri doesn't respond to that. She obviously doesn't want to stop me from sacrificing myself to save her. But it's okay. I don't mind. It's my fault she's in this place anyway. I'd gladly die so she could get out, even if she doesn't love me the same way I love her.

"It'll be weird for the kid," she says.

"What kid?"

"The one watching television. We'll crawl out of the screen into his living room."

I snicker. "Yeah. I guess so. Especially because we'll look like cartoons on this side of the screen." I let out a snicker. "I wonder if we'll get arrested for breaking and entering."

"I hope the kid lives somewhere nice. Like Hawaii or the Bahamas."

"It'll be a long way home from the Bahamas."

She shrugs. "That's fine. I don't mind taking my time."

We continue holding each other, listening to each other breathe, resting in the cold sunlight.

Peri breaks the silence first.

"What is she anyway?" she asks.

"Who? The bunny?"

She nods.

"Berry Bunny. A cereal mascot."

"No, I mean what is she *really*?"

I shake my head. "I don't know. If I had to guess I'd say she's like a spider and this is her web. She feeds on humans. Maybe she feeds on our souls. I don't know exactly."

"What is that Dave said?" she asks. "He said something about the commercial being for the things in the darkness."

"I don't know. He was dying. He wasn't thinking straight."

Peri doesn't pry further, satisfied with my answer. Or maybe she doesn't really want to know for sure.

If I had to guess I'd say he saw something in the darkness. Maybe a gateway to another world. Not our world. Not the cartoon world. But a completely different world, one where its commercials were much different than ours. A world where commercials really happened. They don't film commercials with actors or draw them in cartoons like we do on Earth. When they make a commercial, they create a whole pocket universe where the show can come to life on its own, where everything is completely real. They watch as people are stolen from other worlds and put on display inside of the commercial's universe. What product is being sold, I don't know. Maybe they are selling Fruit Fun cereal. Maybe they are selling a method for turning people into a thousand clones of themselves. I have no idea.

There's a good chance I'll never know.

I get Peri to her feet.

"It's time," I tell her. "We have to go back."

She shivers at the thought, but nods her head in agreement. She knows it's the only way. If we want to get out of the commercial we have to be in that kitchen. We have to wait for a commercial to be broadcast and be there when the gateway opens.

When we get back into the kitchen, Berry Bunny is nowhere in sight, but there is an addition to the breakfast table. A fifth child. This one is much larger than the other children, but just as hideously deformed.

Peri won't look at the cartoon Dave when we enter the kitchen. She won't look at any of them. Like the other children, he doesn't acknowledge us. He just sits there, eating spoonfuls of Fruit Fun cereal.

We can hear the screams of tiny Kims coming from the bowls, but we don't dare look at them. We can't bear the thought of seeing her like that.

For hours, we hide in the kitchen, waiting for Berry Bunny to broadcast the commercial to another poor child's living room. But she doesn't show. We cower behind the counter, listening to the children smacking and gulping, listening to distant Kims screaming and begging for mercy.

"It'll happen," I tell Peri, holding her close to me. "Don't worry. Sooner or later, it will happen."

Then I cover her ears so that she doesn't have to listen to the horrible sounds coming from the breakfast table.

It's been a day or so. I don't know by the fake sun in the frozen sky, but both of us have slept twice, sleeping in shifts.

When Berry Bunny arrives, we take our places.

She steps into the kitchen, surprising the children with two full boxes of her cereal.

"Berry Bunny!" the children cry. "You're back!"

The bunny wiggles her tail at them. "That's right!"

"Did you bring us Fruit Fun cereal?" the little one asks.

"You bet I did!" she says, pouring the cereal into their bowls.

I peek out from my hiding spot, looking at the area around the breakfast table. There isn't anything resembling a screen. No gateway to another world.

"Is it there?" Peri asks in a whisper.

"I don't know," I whisper back.

The bunny pours milk over the fresh bowls of miniature Kims and the children chow down.

"Thank you so much, Berry Bunny!" the Dave child says. "Your cereal is delicious!"

Even though his voice is squeaky and distorted, it still resembles Dave. I wonder if he still has his mind, his memories. I wonder if it really is still Dave or if his body has been taken over by something else. I wonder if he has any control of his actions at all. Or maybe the cereal has just hooked him like a drug, where he is willing to say or do anything to get more. There has to be some kind of magic or some kind of chemical driving him to act the way he does.

"You're welcome, Davy," the bunny says to him, rubbing his head. "But Fruit Fun isn't just delicious. With over thirteen vitamins and minerals, it's also good for you, too!"

As I watch their routine, I realize Berry Bunny often looks at the same spot in a section of the wall behind the children. If there is a screen, that is where it surely would be. But there's no screen in sight. No gateway. But Berry Bunny keeps looking there. She smiles and glares at that spot, as though tormenting a child watching her on the other side.

"I think it's there," I tell Peri.

"Really?" she asks, taking a look for herself. "Where?"

I don't show her. There's nothing to see. I think the gateway is invisible on this side. Only Berry Bunny can see it. But if it's there we can likely get through.

"It's on the wall behind the table," I say. "Do you want to try?"

She nods.

I really hope I'm not wrong. I hope there actually is an unseen portal on that wall. It's a gamble but one we don't have a choice but to take.

"Go!" I whisper.

Then we run out from our hiding place and charge the wall. Peri trips the second she gets to her feet, probably from exhaustion and malnourishment, but I pick her right back up and pull her toward the exit.

"Look, children," Berry Bunny says when she sees us. "We have guests! Maybe they'd like to try some Fruit Fun as well!"

We ignore the brightly-colored freak. We run past her and the breakfast table, running straight into the wall.

"You should try some," Berry Bunny says. "It's delicious!"

The children look at us, crying, "It's delicious! It's delicious!"

We feel the surface of the wall, scanning every inch, trying to find the entrance to the other world.

"Where is it?" Peri cries.

I try not to panic. I try not to accept that I might have just doomed us both.

"Keep looking," I say.

Berry Bunny comes toward us, holding out a bowl of Fruit Fun cereal.

"Just have a bite," the bunny says. "One bite and you'll never go back to any other brand of cereal."

We ignore her, focusing on the wall. It has to be here somewhere, I just know it.

"It's so tasty!" Berry Bunny says. "You don't know what you're missing."

I look back to see the cartoon rabbit staring at me with three miniature Kims dangling from her mouth. She slurps them up through her lips and gulps them down one at a time. Then she closes her eyes and licks her whiskers in satisfaction.

I turn back to the wall. Just one more try. If I don't find it in one more try then I'll give up and take Peri and run.

"Well, if you don't want to *eat* my cereal then maybe you'll help me *make* more of it," says the bunny. "I think you'd both make absolutely delicious bowls of cereal."

As I scan the wall, my finger slips through. Just for a second. But when I feel again, it's no longer there.

"I almost had it," I tell Peri.

It dawns on me. When I watched the cartoon as a child, the screen didn't stay in one place. Like a camera, there were different angles, switching sides of the room from shot to shot. The portal back to our world doesn't stay in one place. It moves.

"Are you ready for more Fruit Fun?" Berry Bunny asks the children.

They hammer their spoons on the table in applause.

"Which kind would you like?" the Bunny asks. "Boy or girl?"

"Boy! Boy!" some of them cry.

"Girl! Girl!" cry the others.

I look at Peri and tell her about my theory. She nods. Then we both feel for the moving gateway as quickly as we can.

"Which one?" Berry Bunny asks. "We'll have to put it to a vote. Raise your hand if you want Boy Fruit Fun."

I don't look back, too busy searching for the exit. So I don't know how many of them raise their hand.

"Now, raise your hand if you want Girl Fruit Fun," says Berry Bunny.

More children raise their hands. We only have seconds. We have to find it.

"Okay, then..." says Berry Bunny.

My hand slides through a hole in the wall.

"I found it!" I yell.

I hold the sides with both of my hands, making sure not to let it go in case it tries to move again.

"Girl it is!" the bunny says.

I put my head through the portal and find myself looking inside somebody's living room. There are three very small children watching the television with big smiles on their faces. They are between the ages of two and four years old. They have no idea what's going on. They just wave at me like it's completely normal for a cartoon character to poke their head out of the television set.

I bring my face back into the commercial and tell Peri, "Let's go."

Before Peri can get to me, the bunny grabs her. She screams and begs for help.

I look at the portal, then back at Peri. If I go through now I could escape. I could get out and save myself. But it would mean sacrificing the woman I love, the woman pregnant with my child. I can't do it. Even if I did get out I wouldn't have been able to live with myself. If only one of us gets out alive it has to be Peri.

"Help me!" Peri cries. "Don't let her change me!"

I run at them. Just before the bunny's hands begin to glow, I grab her by the rubbery pink wrists and pull her away. The energy glows from her palms, but they can't reach Peri. They can do nothing when not touching human skin.

"Let me go, Petey," the bunny says to me. "I haven't

finished breakfast yet."

Peri backs away, her eyes locked on us.

"Run," I tell her, holding the bunny's hands back with all my strength. "Go through the gateway. Get out of here."

But Peri doesn't do that. A look of intensity burns in her eyes. She doesn't want to run. She wants the bunny dead.

"Hold her," Peri tells me.

"Wait…" I say.

I don't know how to stop her. I just do as she asks, holding the bunny in the tightest grip I can muster.

Peri kicks the bunny in the stomach. On impact, the glow leaves the bunny's palms. Peri kicks her again. Then she punches her in the face.

"Stop," I tell her. "You're going to knock her out of my grip."

Peri seems to understand, but she doesn't respond to me. Her eyes are distant, angry. She wants to tear the bunny apart, kill it with her bare hands.

"Don't hurt me," says Berry Bunny. "It's not my fault."

But Peri doesn't listen to her pleas for mercy. She grabs the bunny around the neck and strangles her. The bunny chokes and gags, trying to break out of my grip so that she can turn her attacker into cereal. But I hold on with all my strength. There's no way I'm going to let her go.

"Die!" Peri cries as she strangles her. "Die!"

The children at the table stare at us as we try to

kill their cereal mascot. They don't seem to understand what's going on. They don't do anything to stop us.

"What's wrong, Berry Bunny?" one child asks. "Aren't you going to give us more Fruit Fun cereal?"

"Yeah," another child cries. "You said we'd get more Fruit Fun!"

The strangling doesn't kill the bunny fast enough. Peri releases her grip and lunges at the rabbit. She bites into her neck like a mad dog and tightens her jaws around the bunny's flesh. The rabbit lets out a high-pitched cry as Peri rips out her throat.

"Berry Bunny!" the children cry.

A geyser of purple blood splashes across the wall and the breakfast table as the bunny falls to her knees. Peri isn't done with her. She bites her neck again, ripping off chunks of meat, drinking her purple blood.

"Die!" Peri screams. "Die!"

The light fades from the bunny's eyes. She falls to the ground, plopping onto the tile flooring, rolling over on her back.

We look down at the rabbit. The rabbit looks back up at us.

Before she dies, she says one last thing to us.

She says, "Thank you."

That's all she says. Just *thank you*. It's as though she had been waiting a very long time for someone to come along and put her out of her misery.

"You did it," I tell Peri, looking up at her as she stands over the bunny's corpse.

She doesn't say anything. She just stares at me with a ferocious look in her eyes, purple blood dribbling down her chin.

CHAPTER
EIGHT

With the bunny dead, nothing changes. The curse isn't lifted. The commercial isn't over. Dave and the other children don't go back to their old selves. We aren't sent home. Everything is as it has been.

There's only one thing that changed with the death of Berry Bunny, the only thing we didn't want to have changed—the gateway is closed. There's no way to get back home. We spend hours searching the wall for the exit, but there's nothing there anymore. It's completely gone. And without Berry Bunny, there's no way to open it again.

"What are we going to do?" Peri asks. "We're stuck here."

I don't have an answer for her. Unless we can figure out the technology of the world, figure out how the bunny created the gateway in the first place, if it wasn't just merely magic that did it, then maybe, just maybe, we'd be able to get out. But how long would it take to figure out something like that? It's not like there's a manual for this kind of thing.

"We should look outside," I say.

"But there's not going to be a gateway out there," she says. "You said so yourself."

"No, we're not looking for a gateway," I say. "We want to find out where the bunny lives."

"What do you mean?" she asks.

"The bunny has to live somewhere out there. We have to find out where. There might be something in her home that will help us get out of here."

Although she doesn't seem very confident in the plan, Peri agrees.

We spend hours searching the neighborhood, going from house to house, seeing if any of the doors open. There's a chance one of these houses is as real as the one with the breakfast table. We just have to find the right one.

"Wait a minute," Peri says. "Bunnies don't live inside of houses. They live in rabbit holes."

I nod at her. "Yeah, you might be right. Let's look for holes in the ground."

We search in backyards and patches of fake grass. The hole is at the foot of the largest tree in the neighborhood, only a couple houses down from the main house.

Standing over the rabbit hole, we look down, staring into the abyss.

"Ready?" I ask.

Peri nods.

Then we climb down, into the rabbit's home.

Beneath the ground, we enter a large warm dwelling. The walls look like they're made of dirt, but they're plastic, just as fake as everything else in the world.

"There's nothing here," Peri says.

She's right. In the corner of the room is a bed of hay. On the far wall are shelves full of empty Fruit Fun cereal boxes. There are spoons and bowls and a table with a single chair at it where Berry Bunny must have eaten breakfast most days, when she wasn't eating with the children. Besides all of this, there's nothing here that can help us.

We keep looking anyway, digging through cereal boxes, looking under the bed.

I wonder what the rabbit used to do down here, when she wasn't making Fruit Fun commercials or tormenting children. I wonder if she had hobbies or dreams. I wonder if she had family and friends. I wonder if she wasn't just a horrible, demonic robot programmed to trap children inside its web.

After we search every inch, finding nothing that can help us, we decide to give up.

"We're never going home, are we?" Peri asks.

I look at her and frown. I don't want to lie to her. I don't think it looks very good for us.

She wraps her arms around me and I hug her close. I press my forehead against hers.

"I'm sorry," Peri says. "If you didn't come back for me you could have escaped. You could have been free."

I shake my head. "No way. I'd never leave you."

She looks me in the eyes. "Really?"

I nod. "Not in a million years. I would rather die than let anything bad happen to you. I would rather be stuck here for the rest of my life."

Peri smiles at me, but she forces the smile like she doesn't want to be rude.

"I don't care what happens next," I say to her. "I'm just happy that I'm with you."

I hug her close to me, pressing her face to my chest. Her muscles are tense and awkward.

"You mean everything to me," I continue. "I'd do anything to make you happy."

Then she kisses me. She kisses me deeper and more passionately than she ever has before, more than *anyone* has before. It all feels like an act, but I don't care. I let my doubts slip away. I kiss her back. She holds me tightly, pulling me into her bosom, sucking my tongue into her mouth. My heart flutters. My skin becomes gooseflesh. My hairs stand on end. My body becomes warm with her love. I've never felt so close to another human being as I do with her now.

When our lips part, I say, "I love you."

She says, "I love you, too."

Her warmth continues flowing through me. It goes from my heart down to my toes, up to my head, across my arms to my fingertips. It's like her love is flowing from her body directly into mine.

But then her warmth becomes even warmer. It becomes so warm that it burns.

I look down. Her hands are glowing against my waist. The glow has spread across my body, covering my skin. It's the same glow that came from Berry Bunny's palms when she transformed Kim.

Peri opens her eyes and sees what she's doing. She had no idea what was happening. Her mouth drops open in shock. Somehow Berry Bunny's power has been transferred to her. Maybe because Peri killed her or maybe because she swallowed some of her blood. Whatever the case, she can do exactly what the bunny could do. She can turn people into human cereal.

"Pete!" Peri cries.

She pulls her hands away from me, but it's too late. I feel my body already splintering, separating.

I hug her tightly to me one last time before I crumble into pieces. I become a blanket of tiny people wrapped around Peri's body, pouring out of my clothes, piling into a giant pool at her feet, sliding down her chest like an avalanche down a mountain side.

Being a mass of clones of myself is different than I thought it would be. I can see out of the eyes of every version of me. I can feel what they feel. Think what they think. Speak through a thousand different mouths. It's like I still have only one consciousness inhabiting hundreds of different bodies.

Peri collects all of me and puts me into Berry Bunny's bed.

"I'm sorry," she says, looking down at me with her massive round head. "I didn't know…"

Tears roll down her eyes and splash onto some of my clones, drenching them like somebody poured a warm bucket of salt water over their heads.

"It's okay," I say through a thousand tiny mouths. "It's not your fault."

"What am I supposed to do?" she asks.

I feel my new pink skin. It's firm and slightly crispy. My hair is thick sugary strands, the texture of cotton candy. Even though it is horrible finding myself in this state, I don't blame Peri. She didn't know.

"This might be a good thing," I say, trying to think on the bright side. "If you have Berry Bunny's powers, maybe you also have the power to open the portal back to our world. Maybe you have the power to make me whole again."

"Well, how do I know if I do or not?" she asks.

"Just concentrate. Focus. Act on any instinct that comes over you. I'm sure you'll figure it out sooner or later."

Peri smiles and nods at me.

"Okay," she says. "I'll try."

Peri and I spend the next several days trying to get her to figure out how to open the doorway to our world. But it doesn't seem to work. She has no idea how she even transformed me. She doesn't know if she'll ever be able to control her powers.

"Just use your instincts," I say through all my mouths. I sound like a swarm of cricket people. "You'll figure it out."

"I'll never figure it out!" she cries, slamming her fist down onto the bed with frustration. The impact sends two of my clones bouncing into the air.

Then she leaves the rabbit hole and goes for a walk. It's what she always does. She's been getting crankier and crankier every day.

Peri hasn't just been getting crankier every day. She's also been changing, transforming. After a few days of killing Berry Bunny, her skin turned pink. Then she developed purple spots. Now her hair is falling out and large ears are growing in. She doesn't wear clothes anymore, walking around the rabbit hole in the nude, exposing her brightly colored cartoon flesh.

"Just envision yourself opening a portal," I say to her.

She groans at me. "Shut the fuck up! That's all you

ever say. It doesn't help. Ever."

"But you have to try," my clones say. "I'm sure if you keep trying it'll come to you."

She rolls her large eyes. "I *have* been trying. I'm just too hungry to concentrate."

Peri ran out of the normal cereal days ago, scarfing down every pink ball that was left in the commercial world. She's down to just drinking milk. For some reason, I don't need food anymore. I'm never hungry. I'm never thirsty. So I let Peri have all the last of the food.

"Maybe you can figure out how to make more food," I tell her. "The pink ball kind."

"You think I haven't been trying that?" she asks, sneering at me.

She paces the room, digging deep into the back of her mind, but the answers aren't inside of her. Not yet anyway.

"God damnit," Peri cries, throwing her arms up in frustration. "Fuck this. I can't do it anymore."

"Of course you can," I say.

"No, I can't," she says. "I'm just too hungry."

Then she stomps toward me, looking down at me with frustration.

"It's just too much," she says.

She puts a cereal bowl against the edge of the bed and brushes three handfuls of me inside.

"What are you doing?" I cry at her through a dozen mouths.

"I'm just going to eat some of you," she says, her voice cranky at me.

I shriek, jumping up and down in her bowl. "What! You can't do that!"

"You said you'd do *anything* for me," she says in an annoyed tone, imitating the way I said those words to her days ago.

"No," I cry. "Peri, please don't."

She doesn't understand. I experience what every little piece of me experiences. If she eats some of me she'll put all of me through horrible agony. Like eating somebody's leg while it's still attached to them. I try telling her that it will hurt. I try telling her that she might end up like Dave after he ate the pieces of Kim cereal. But she doesn't listen to me. Her mind is made up.

She puts the bowl of me onto the bunny's breakfast table. Then she pours milk over my heads.

"I'm sorry," she says, peering down into the bowl with her giant pink head. "I'll be able to focus better after I eat."

Swimming in the pool of milk, it feels weird against my body. It's soft, soothing.

She says, "I won't eat anymore of you after this. I promise."

The milk around me turns pink. I don't understand it at first. Where is the pink milk coming from? But then I realize it's me. I'm turning it pink. The milk is making me soggy, melting my skin. My cotton candy hair dissolves from my heads.

"Please, Peri," I say to her, looking up into her big bulging eyes. "You can't do this. I'm melting in here."

She takes a scoop of me, cradling five of me inside a puddle of milk in her spoon, lifting me toward her mouth. Once she looks at me inside of the spoon, just inches from her lips, she pauses. She finally realizes what she is doing.

"I'm sorry…" she says.

A tear forms in her eye.

But even though she's sorry, she doesn't change her mind. She's beyond the point of no return. She's already decided to go through with it.

She opens her mouth, revealing a deep purple cavern. Then she guides me within. I can hear deep gurgling sounds echo from the depths of her throat, the sound of her rolling tongue smacking against her teeth like a slimy red whale swimming beneath us. She closes her lips around the spoon and sucks all five of me off, pink milk and all. Her tongue presses me against the roof of her mouth. My skin melts in her saliva as it had in the milk. I can feel her taste buds peeling off layers of flesh. But it doesn't hurt. It just feels like I'm washing lathered soap from my body.

Other versions of me look up, staring at Peri as she tastes the first five. She lifts back her head, pulling me to the back of her throat with her tongue. Then she swallows. My flesh is squeezed and melted, leaving a pink trail down her esophagus. Once I'm inside her stomach, I don't last very long. The squishy pulsing organ is hungry and ferocious. The walls rub against my tiny bodies, melting them into goo almost immediately. Just before my vision fades, I notice that her stomach has changed just as much as her outer body. It doesn't look like a human stomach—it's smooth-textured and glows bright pink, more like something from a cartoon.

Watching Peri from the bowl, her eyes are still closed, her mouth becomes a frown. Then she sobs at the tops of her lungs. Tears pour from her eyes. Her mouth wide open as she bawls out loud.

I figure she must now realize what a horrible thing she just did. She must realize how cruel and selfish and brutal it was. But that's not it all. She's not crying with despair. She's crying with joy.

"You're…so…good…" she says between sobs.

She takes another bite of me, scooping seven up this time.

After she swallows these versions of me, she sighs. "I love you so much."

Then she really digs in. She scoops pieces of me into her mouth as fast as she can, gulping down every clone that passes her lips.

"More," she says. "I need more."

When she finishes the bowl of me, she goes back to the bed and gets a refill, pulling twice as many of my bodies inside.

"What are you doing?" I cry. "You said you wouldn't eat anymore after that."

But she doesn't listen. She doesn't even look down

in the bowl at me as she gobbles me down, moaning and sobbing with joy. When she's done with this bowl, she goes back and gets another. And then another. Until her belly is so full it looks like an inflated pink beach ball with purple polka dots down the sides.

She rubs her stomach like she's just had the best meal of her life. Then she walks to the bed and lays down. All of my bodies move out of the way so that she doesn't crush them.

When she opens her eyes and sees me staring at her, all of my hundreds of eyes fuming with anger, she just groans at me.

"Oh, stop whining," she says. "There's still plenty of you left."

Then she rolls over, facing away from me, and goes to sleep.

CHAPTER
NINE

Time passes. It seems like it's been weeks or months. Peri becomes more like Berry Bunny every day. As a joke, she asks me to start calling her Peary Bunny.

"My cereal tastes more like pear than berry anyway," she says.

I'm guessing that I'm the cereal she's talking about.

Her ears have grown past her shoulders. Her butt has sprouted a large fluffy tail. Her eyes are wide and cartoonish. Her feet are long and fuzzy. She has become the same race as Berry Bunny, but she still looks a lot like Peri. I can still see my girlfriend in her eyes, in her smile. She's not turning into the same monstrous cartoon mascot. She's got her own mind. She's got her own will. No matter what she looks like, she's still my Peri.

But, unfortunately, her being Peri is bad enough. Like she was back in the real world, Peri is not very considerate. She's more interested in herself, more interested in doing what makes her happy even if I get screwed over in the process.

She continues eating bowls of me. She says I'm just too delicious not to. She says that I'm an important part of a balanced breakfast.

"You have to stop eating me like this," I tell her from the cereal bowl. "You're eating too much."

But she always gets mad at me when I argue with her about it.

In an aggravated tone, she says, "I'm sorry, but I'm pregnant. I'm eating for two."

She keeps saying this as an excuse to eat more bowls of me than she needs to, just because she's growing addicted to the flavor. I don't think she even is pregnant anymore. Her belly doesn't look like she's getting pregnant. She's not lactating. I think her transformation into the cartoon mascot has somehow terminated the pregnancy.

At night, she sleeps with me in the bunny bed, wrapping all of the pieces of me over her like a blanket. She's only crushed a couple of me so far. She's usually very gentle. But as the days go by, and she continues eating cereal bowl after cereal bowl, the blanket of me has become small and smaller. I'm just barely a dishrag-sized sheet covering a small section of her hip.

She says she's getting close to being able to open a portal to the other world. Somewhere in her mind, the information is forming, surging to the surface of her brain like an old memory. She thinks she'll be able to open it for sure soon. But in the meantime, I'm being quickly eaten away. There's not likely going to be a way she'll be able to return me to my formal self. She'll likely not be able to change herself back either. But if she can open the doorway, at least there's a chance she'll be able to save herself. She might look freakish being a pink and purple bunny out in the real world, but at least she'll be free. At least she'll be able to have some kind of a normal life, even if people assume she's wearing a Halloween costume all the time.

Peri becomes less and less herself as the days progress. She forgets things sometimes. She starts acting more and more like the Berry Bunny from the commercials. Whenever she eats me, she doesn't treat me as her boyfriend anymore. She just treats me like cereal, commenting on my delicious taste and nutrition. She keeps the majority of me inside of cereal boxes on the shelf, leaving only a single clone out on the bed so that she has one of me to talk to. I have to constantly snap her out of it, remind her of who she really is.

One day, while we're sitting together at the small breakfast table, she gets up from her chair and says, "I think I've got it."

"What?" I ask.

"The gateway…" she says. "All I have to do is open it in my mind."

I jump up and down on the table in excitement. "Do it then! Do it!"

"I have to find a television somewhere…" she says,

her eyes glazing over. "Someone has to be watching…"

It seems like she's scanning the screens of millions of televisions at once, trying to pick the perfect one.

"It doesn't matter who," I say. "Just pick one. Any of them."

"The children are easiest," she says. "Their minds are more open."

"Just do it," I cry.

Then a window opens up on the wall in front of us. I can see the gateway this time. Peri can control its visibility. A 72 inch rectangle forms before us, revealing a large living room. A small boy sits there, watching us like a television show, eating grasshopper cookies and milk.

Peri looks down on me.

"Go," I tell her. "Don't worry about me, just go."

"I want to take you with me," she says.

"There's nothing for me out there," I say. "I'm too small to have any kind of a life. You should go without me. Just go while the portal's still open."

Peri looks at the gateway, then down at me.

"I love you…" she says.

Then her eyes change, her personality dissipates, the bunny takes over.

"…my delicious piece of cereal," she continues.

I try to snap her out of it. "Peri! Not now! You have to get out of here!"

She looks at the television screen and smiles at the child.

"Hi kids, I'm Peary Bunny!" she says. "Are you

hungry for breakfast?"

She takes a box of me from the shelf and pours herself a bowl, putting on a show for the child on the other side of the screen.

Covering me in milk, she scoops spoonfuls of me up into her mouth. "Try some of my Fruit Fun cereal! It's *peary* delicious!"

As she scoops me into her mouth, one bite at a time, I yell at her, trying to bring her back to reality. "Peri! It's me! Remember who you are! I'm not cereal! I'm your boyfriend!"

The bunny takes two more bites before she realizes what she's doing. She drops the spoon back into the bowl.

"Pete?" she asks. Tears fall from her eyes. "What am I doing? Why am I eating you?"

"You need to escape," I say.

She looks up at the television screen.

"Go now," I say. "Get out before it's too late."

She nods and sets the bowl down. She picks up one of me, the dry one that didn't end up getting soggy in milk, and puts it in her bra.

"Okay," she says.

She turns to the television screen. The little boy just stares at us, eating his cookies, trying to figure out the plot of this cartoon.

"Bye little Petes," she says to those of me she's leaving behind.

Then she grabs onto the side of the television set and crawls through the portal. The boy on the other side of the screen drops the cookie in his hand, spills his milk across the carpet. His mouth droops open.

As Peri crawls out of the screen, she smiles at the boy, tries to calm him down.

"It's okay," she says. "I'm not going to hurt you."

She climbs further.

"I just need to use your television for a few minutes and then I'll leave," she says.

The boy nods, completely trusting the cartoon rabbit as it crawls into his living room.

"Who are you?" he asks.

"I'm..." Peri says. "I'm Pe—" Her eyes glaze over again. "I'm Peary Bunny! You're just going to love my Fruit Fun cereal!"

As the bunny crawls forward, the boy inches away.

"Come try some!" she says.

The boy screams as the bunny grabs him and pulls him back into the television set. Once they are completely inside, the gateway to the real world closes behind them. Peri grabs the boy with both palms, filling him with a glowing energy. The boy immediately crumbles into miniature clones of himself.

I watch in horror as the bunny who was once my girlfriend fills empty cereal boxes with the pieces of the child. Then she pours a bowl of him, dumping him on top of the leftovers of me now gone soggy in the milk. The little boy screams in my ear as she eats us with delight.

There are no longer any signs of Peri in the bunny's eyes. The Peri I knew is gone, giving herself over to the commercial. She's now just Peary Bunny, and I am nothing but Fruit Fun to her.

CHAPTER
TEN

"I wish I had something healthy and delicious," says a little cartoon boy sitting at a breakfast table, frowning, his plump cheeks resting in his hands.

"I wish I had some Fruit Fun cereal," says Davy, grumbling and flicking his spoon.

"Maybe Berry Bunny will bring us some," says Milly, trying to cheer up the other children at the table.

"But Berry Bunny's dead…" says little Robby, his frown growing deeper. "We'll never get any more Fruit Fun cereal…"

A cartoon bunny hops into the kitchen and says, "Did somebody say Fruit Fun cereal?"

The children explode with joy.

"Who are you?" asks Milly.

"You're not Berry Bunny!" cries little Robby.

"Nope," the bunny says. She puts a cowboy hat on her head. "I'm her Texan cousin, *Peary* Bunny!"

"Peary Bunny?" the children ask with confused yet cheerful voices.

"That's right," she says. "And I'm here with my brand

new Prickly Pear Fruit Fun, the rootin' tootin' taste of the southwest!"

Then she makes pistols with her fingers and fires them into the air.

"Prickly Pear Fruit Fun?" they shout with excitement. "That sounds yummy!"

"Try some," she says.

Peary Bunny pours boxes of tiny pink children into their bowls and fills it with milk. The cartoons dig in, gobbling down the little people.

"This is amazing, Peary Bunny!" Milly cries.

After gulping down a few wiggling morsels, Davy says, "Your Prickly Pear Fruit Fun is the tastiest!"

"It's not only tasty," Peary Bunny says, as she pours herself a bowl. "It's also good for you, too! It's an important part of a balanced breakfast!"

The last of me falls out of the box into Peary Bunny's bowl. There's nothing left. Just twenty clones, not even enough to fill her cereal bowl. She pours milk over the tops of my heads. Then scoops a heaping spoonful and forces me into her big wet cartoon maw. One of me sticks to the side of her lip, my legs and arms wiggling in the air, before she licks me up and swallows me with the others.

"Mmm…" she says. "Isn't it delicious? It's got the sweet and tangy zip of real prickly pear cactus fruit!"

The children nod their heads in agreement as they gorge themselves on the prickly pear cereal.

"It's always a fun time with Fruit Fun."

Peri no longer recognizes me as she looks down into the bowl. She scoops me up one morsel at a time and swallows me into a soggy pile of mushed-together clones, churning me within her wet pink digestion chamber that smells of sweet artificial fruit flavoring and rotting human flesh.

As she eats me, I just surrender to my fate. There's nothing I can do to stop it now that I'm just a dozen or so tiny pieces of melting cereal in her bowl. I still love Peri. Even though she's become a monster, even though she's eating me alive, I still love her. And it makes me happy that she finally loves me, too. She might only love me for my sweet fruit flavor. She might only love me for my vitamins and minerals. She might only love me when I fill her belly with delicious nourishment. But, in a way, it is still love. Eating me makes her happy. And I've never brought her more happiness than I do now, hugging my tiny pink bodies against her slimy cartoon tongue.

Peary Bunny turns to the television screen, peering into a living room where three children gather to watch the cereal commercial.

"Would you like to try some of my Prickly Pear Fruit Fun?" she asks them.

She takes the last spoonful of me and drives it through the screen into their world. The children look down at me in the spoon, my flesh melting into the pink milk, my eyes blinking up at them. I want to warn them to stay away. I want to tell them all about the horrible world on this side of the television. I want to ask them to call my fathers and tell them I love them. But as I open my mouths to speak, only milk dribbles out. My tongues are just puddles of goo between my crispy teeth.

"Don't want any?" Peary Bunny asks the children. "Fine. Suit yourself."

Then she puts the spoon into her mouth. She swallows the last of me with a loud gulp and then lets out a sigh of satisfaction.

"More for me," she says.

From within her overly stuffed belly, pressed tightly against the side of her pulsing stomach by a blob of mushy pink flesh, I hear the children scream and run from the room to get their parents.

For their sake, for their parents' sake, even for the sake of Peri's immortal soul—if she still even has one—I hope they never turn on another television set for the rest of their lives.

On this side of the screen, there's nothing but a floppy pink spider waiting to wrap you up in her sticky, milky web. And once she has you, she'll never let you go… especially if you never want her to.

BONUS SECTION

This is the part of the book where we would have published an afterword by the author but he insisted on drawing a comic strip instead for reasons we don't quite understand.

I hope you liked my new book *Spider Bunny*.

Wasn't it sugary?

It's me CM3!

I dedicate this book to my friend, Simon Oré.

Simon

Simon is a development executive at Starburns Industries Animation Studios, founder of SBI Comics, and was a producer on the Charlie Kaufman film *Anomalisa*. He is also the president of The Cinefamily theatre in LA and is trying to get a bunch of my books adapted to film, like *Ultra Fuckers* and *Zombies and Shit*.

Why *Spider Bunny* is dedicated to Simon is because he's addicted to kids' cereals. Even kids don't eat as much kids' cereal as Simon does.

In fact, I bet he'd eat nothing but cereal for every meal of every day if it wouldn't kill him.

CRUNCH Berries

CORN FLAKES

LUCKY Charms

Fact: after you turn thirty, children's cereals are basically just diabetes in a box.

Simon often throws cereal parties, where he invites all of his friends to his place to dress in pajamas, watch a bunch of old Saturday morning cartoons and eat bowls upon bowls of Apple Jacks, Cookie Crisp, and Fruity Pebbles until they're lying on the floor twitching from the sugar overdose.

He also introduced this concept to The Cinefamily, where they play retro cartoons on the big screen and everyone in the audience dresses in pajamas and eats kids' cereals.

Besides eating the cereal, he also likes to collect the prizes he finds at the bottoms of the cereal boxes.

Over the years, he has amassed a vast assortment of wacky wall walkers, super bouncy balls, puffy stickers, temporary tattoos, iron-on patches, and various small plastic toys.

But one time he found an especially unusual prize at the bottom of a cereal box.

It was a living, breathing miniature version of himself.

He didn't know what to make of the tiny Simon. The little version of him just stood there, looking up with a creepy smile on his face.

They tried communicating but Tiny Simon only spoke a weird alien language he couldn't understand.

So they decided to just hang out and eat cereal together.

Note: Tiny Simon is so small that he only needs to eat a single piece of cereal.

At first, it was a perfect relationship.

Simon took Tiny Simon everywhere he went.

They flew kites on the beach.

They watched cartoons at The Cinefamily.

They even went on double dates together.

But after a while, Simon realized there was something very off about his tiny doppelganger.

Perhaps it was the way he stared at him whenever he was masturbating.

Or how he disintegrated random people with a miniature death ray gun whenever he was bored.

Simon wondered if it was possible to get rid of the tiny version of himself.

So, one day, he gave his clone a large helium balloon.

And Tiny Simon floated off into space.

He's not been seen or heard from since.

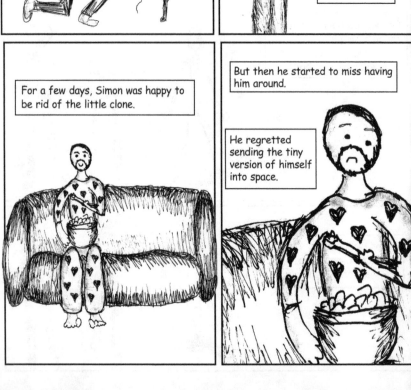

For a few days, Simon was happy to be rid of the little clone.

But then he started to miss having him around.

He regretted sending the tiny version of himself into space.

ABOUT THE AUTHOR

Carlton Mellick III is one of the leading authors of the bizarro fiction subgenre. Since 2001, his books have drawn an international cult following, despite the fact that they have been shunned by most libraries and chain bookstores.

He won the Wonderland Book Award for his novel, *Warrior Wolf Women of the Wasteland*, in 2009. His short fiction has appeared in *Vice Magazine, The Year's Best Fantasy and Horror #16, The Magazine of Bizarro Fiction,* and *Zombies: Encounters with the Hungry Dead*, among others. He is also a graduate of Clarion West, where he studied under the likes of Chuck Palahniuk, Connie Willis, and Cory Doctorow.

He lives in Portland, OR, the bizarro fiction mecca.

Visit him online at **www.carltonmellick.com**

QUICKSAND HOUSE

Tick and Polly have never met their parents before. They live in the same house with them, they dream about them every night, they share the same flesh and blood, yet for some reason their parents have never found the time to visit them even once since they were born. Living in a dark corner of their parents' vast crumbling mansion, the children long for the day when they will finally be held in their mother's loving arms for the first time... But that day seems to never come. They worry their parents have long since forgotten about them.

When the machines that provide them with food and water stop functioning, the children are forced to venture out of the nursery to find their parents on their own. But the rest of the house is much larger and stranger than they ever could have imagined. The maze-like hallways are dark and seem to go on forever, deranged creatures lurk in every shadow, and the bodies of long-dead children litter the abandoned storerooms. Every minute out of the nursery is a constant battle for survival. And the deeper into the house they go, the more they must unravel the mysteries surrounding their past and the world they've grown up in, if they ever hope to meet the parents they've always longed to see.

Like a survival horror rendition of *Flowers in the Attic*, Carlton Mellick III's *Quicksand House* is his most gripping and sincere work to date.

HUNGRY BUG

In a world where magic exists, spell-casting has become a serious addiction. It ruins lives, tears families apart, and eats away at the fabric of society. Those who cast too much are taken from our world, never to be heard from again. They are sent to a realm known as Hell's Bottom—a sorcerer ghetto where everyday life is a harsh struggle for survival. Porcelain dolls crawl through the alleys like rats, arcane scientists abduct people from the streets to use in their ungodly experiments, and everyone lives in fear of the aristocratic race of spider people who prey on citizens like vampires.

Told in a series of interconnected stories reminiscent of Frank Miller's *Sin City* and David Lapham's *Stray Bullets*, Carlton Mellick III's *Hungry Bug* is an urban fairy tale that focuses on the real life problems that arise within a fantastic world of magic.

SWEET STORY

Sally is an odd little girl. It's not because she dresses as if she's from the Edwardian era or spends most of her time playing with creepy talking dolls. It's because she chases rainbows as if they were butterflies. She believes that if she finds the end of the rainbow then magical things will happen to her--leprechauns will shower her with gold and fairies will grant her every wish. But when she actually does find the end of a rainbow one day, and is given the opportunity to wish for whatever she wants, Sally asks for something that she believes will bring joy to children all over the world. She wishes that it would rain candy forever. She had no idea that her innocent wish would lead to the extinction of all life on earth.

TUMOR FRUIT

Eight desperate castaways find themselves stranded on a mysterious deserted island. They are surrounded by poisonous blue plants and an ocean made of acid. Ravenous creatures lurk in the toxic jungle. The ghostly sound of crying babies can be heard on the wind.

Once they realize the rescue ships aren't coming, the eight castaways must band together in order to survive in this inhospitable environment. But survival might not be possible. The air they breathe is lethal, there is no shelter from the elements, and the only food they have to consume is the colorful squid-shaped tumors that grow from a mentally disturbed woman's body.

AS SHE STABBED ME GENTLY IN THE FACE

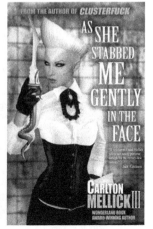

Oksana Maslovskiy is an award-winning artist, an internationally adored fashion model, and one of the most infamous serial killers this country has ever known. She enjoys murdering pretty young men with a nine-inch blade, cutting them open and admiring their delicate insides. It's the only way she knows how to be intimate with another human being. But one day she meets a victim who cannot be killed. His name is Gabriel—a mysterious immortal being with a deep desire to save Oksana's soul. He makes her a deal: if she promises to never kill another person again, he'll become her eternal murder victim.

What at first seems like the perfect relationship for Oksana quickly devolves into a living nightmare when she discovers that Gabriel enjoys being killed by her just a little too much. He turns out to be obsessive, possessive, and paranoid that she might be murdering other men behind his back. And because he is unkillable, it's not going to be easy for Oksana to get rid of him.

CUDDLY HOLOCAUST

Teddy bears, dollies, and little green soldiers—they've all ha
enough of you. They're sick of being treated like playthings fo
spoiled little brats. They have no rights, no property, no hope fo
a future of any kind. You've left them with no other option–i
order to be free, they must exterminate the human race.

Julie is a human girl undergoing reconstructive surgery in orde
to become a stuffed animal. Her plan: to infiltrate enemy line
in order to save her family from the toy death camps. Bu
when an army of plushy soldiers invade the underground
bunker where she has taken refuge, Julie will be forced te
move forward with her plan despite her transformation
being not entirely complete.

ARMADILLO FISTS

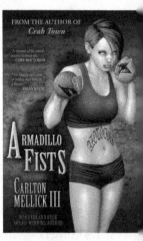

A weird-as-hell gangster story set in a world where people drive
giant mechanical dinosaurs instead of cars.

Her name is Psycho June Howard, aka Armadillo Fists, a
woman who replaced both of her hands with living armadillos.
She was once the most bloodthirsty fighter in the world of
illegal underground boxing. But now she is on the run from a
group of psychotic gangsters who believe she's responsible for
the death of their boss. With the help of a stegosaurus driver
named Mr. Fast Awesome—who thinks he is God's gift to
women even though he doesn't have any arms or legs--June
must do whatever it takes to escape her pursuers, even if she
has to kill each and every one of them in the process.

VILLAGE OF THE MERMAIDS

Mermaids are protected by the government under the Endan-
gered Species Act, which means you aren't able to kill them ever
in self-defense. This is especially problematic if you happen to
live in the isolated fishing village of Siren Cove, where there exists a healthy population of mermaids in the surrounding waters
that view you as the main source of protein in their diet.

The only thing keeping these ravenous sea women at bay
is the equally-dangerous supply of human livestock known as
Food People. Normally, these "feeder humans" are enough to
keep the mermaid population happy and well-fed. But in Siren
Cove, the mermaids are avoiding the human livestock and have
returned to hunting the frightened local fishermen. It is up to
Doctor Black, an eccentric representative of the Food People
Corporation, to investigate the matter and hopefully find a way
to correct the mermaids' new eating patterns before the remain-
ing villagers end up as fish food. But the more he digs, the more
he discovers there are far stranger and more dangerous things
than mermaids hidden in this ancient village by the sea.

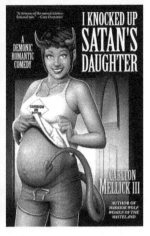

I KNOCKED UP SATAN'S DAUGHTER

Jonathan Vandervoo lives a carefree life in a house made of legos, spending his days building lego sculptures and his nights getting drunk with his only friend—an alcoholic sumo wrestler named Shoji. It's a pleasant life with no responsibility, until the day he meets Lici. She's a soul-sucking demon from hell with red skin, glowing eyes, a forked tongue, and pointy red devil horns... and she claims to be nine months pregnant with Jonathan's baby.

Now Jonathan must do the right thing and marry the succubus or else her demonic family is going to rip his heart out through his ribcage and force him to endure the worst torture hell has to offer for the rest of eternity. But can Jonathan really love a fire-breathing, frog-eating, cold-blooded demoness? Or would eternal damnation be preferable? Either way, the big day is approaching. And once Jonathan's conservative Christian family learns their son is about to marry a spawn of Satan, it's going to be all-out war between demons and humans, with Jonathan and his hell-born bride caught in the middle.

KILL BALL

In a city where everyone lives inside of plastic bubbles, there is no such thing as intimacy. A husband can no longer kiss his wife. A mother can no longer hug her children. To do this would mean instant death. Ever since the disease swept across the globe, we have become isolated within our own personal plastic prison cells, rolling aimlessly through rubber streets in what are essentially man-sized hamster balls.

Colin Hinchcliff longs for the touch of another human being. He can't handle the loneliness, the confinement, and he's horribly claustrophobic. The only thing keeping him going is his unrequited love for an exotic dancer named Siren, a woman who has never seen his face, doesn't even know his name. But when The Kill Ball, a serial slasher in a black leather sphere, begins targeting women at Siren's club, Colin decides he has to do whatever it takes in order to protect her... even if

he has to break out of his bubble and risk everything to do it.

THE TICK PEOPLE

They call it Gloom Town, but that isn't its real name. It is a sad city, the saddest of cities, a place so utterly depressing that even their ales are brewed with the most sorrow-filled tears. They built it on the back of a colossal mountain-sized animal, where its woeful citizens live like human fleas within the hairy, pulsing landscape. And those tasked with keeping the city in a state of constant melancholy are the Stressmen-a team of professional sadness-makers who are perpetually striving to invent new ways of causing absolute misery.

But for the Stressman known as Fernando Mendez, creating grief hasn't been so easy as of late. His ideas aren't effective anymore. His treatments are more likely to induce happiness than sadness. And if he wants to get back in the game, he's going to have to relearn the true meaning of despair.

THE HAUNTED VAGINA

It's difficult to love a woman whose vagina is a gateway to the world of the dead...

Steve is madly in love with his eccentric girlfriend, Stacy. Unfortunately, their sex life has been suffering as of late, because Steve is worried about the odd noises that have been coming from Stacy's pubic region. She says that her vagina is haunted. She doesn't think it's that big of a deal. Steve, on the other hand, completely disagrees.

When a living corpse climbs out of her during an awkward night of sex, Stacy learns that her vagina is actually a doorway to another world. She persuades Steve to climb inside of her to explore this strange new place. But once inside, Steve finds it difficult to return... especially once he meets an oddly attractive woman named Fig, who lives within the lonely haunted world between Stacy's legs.

THE CANNIBALS OF CANDYLAND

There exists a race of cannibals who are made out of candy. They live in an underground world filled with lollipop forests and gumdrop goblins. During the day, while you are away at work, they come above ground and prowl our streets for food. Their prey: your children. They lure young boys and girls to them with their sweet scent and bright colorful candy coating, then rip them apart with razor sharp teeth and claws.

When he was a child, Franklin Pierce witnessed the death of his siblings at the hands of a candy woman with pink cotton candy hair. Since that day, the candy people have become his obsession. He has spent his entire life trying to prove that they exist. And after discovering the entrance to the underground world of the candy people, Franklin finds himself venturing into their sugary domain. His mission: capture one of them and bring it back, dead or alive.

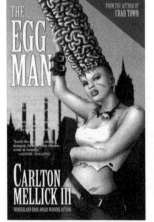

THE EGG MAN

It is a survival of the fittest world where humans reproduce like insects, children are the property of corporations, and having a ten-foot tall brain is a grotesque sexual fetish.

Lincoln has just been released into the world by the Georges Organization, a corporation that raises creative types. A Smell, he has little prospect of succeeding as a visual artist. But after he moves into the Henry Building, he meets Luci, the weird and grimy girl who lives across the hall. She is a Sight. She is also the most disgusting woman Lincoln has ever met. Little does he know, she will soon become his muse.

Now Luci's boyfriend is threatening to kill Lincoln, two rival corporations are preparing for war, and Luci is dragging him along to discover the truth about the mysterious egg man who lives next door. Only the strongest will survive in this tale of individuality, love, and mutilation.

APESHIT

Apeshit is Mellick's love letter to the great and terrible B-horror movie genre. Six trendy teenagers (three cheerleaders and three football players) go to an isolated cabin in the mountains for a weekend of drinking, partying, and crazy sex, only to find themselves in the middle of a life and death struggle against a horribly mutated psychotic freak that just won't stay dead. Mellick parodies this horror cliché and twists it into something deeper and stranger. It is the literary equivalent of a grindhouse film. It is a splatter punk's wet dream. It is perhaps one of the most fucked up books ever written.

If you are a fan of Takashi Miike, Evil Dead, early Peter Jackson, or Eurotrash horror, then you must read this book.

CLUSTERFUCK

A bunch of douchebag frat boys get trapped in a cave with subterranean cannibal mutants and try to survive not by using their wits but by following the bro code...

From master of bizarro fiction Carlton Mellick III, author of the international cult hits Satan Burger and Adolf in Wonderland, comes a violent and hilarious B movie in book form. Set in the same woods as Mellick's splatterpunk satire Apeshit, Clusterfuck follows Trent Chesterton, alpha bro, who has come up with what he thinks is a flawless plan to get laid. He invites three hot chicks and his three best bros on a weekend of extreme cave diving in a remote area known as Turtle Mountain, hoping to impress the ladies with his expert caving skills.

But things don't quite go as Trent planned. For starters, only one of the three chicks turns out to be remotely hot and she has no interest in him for some inexplicable reason. Then he ends up looking like a total dumbass when everyone learns he's never actually gone caving in his entire life. And to top it all off, he's the one to get blamed once they find themselves lost and trapped deep underground with no way to turn back and no possible chance of rescue. What's a bro to do? Sure he could win some points if he actually tried to save the ladies from the family of unkillable subterranean cannibal mutants hunting them for their flesh, but fuck that. No slam piece is worth that amount of effort. He'd much rather just use them as bait so that he can save himself.

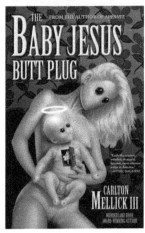

THE BABY JESUS BUTT PLUG

Step into a dark and absurd world where human beings are slaves to corporations, people are photocopied instead of born, and the baby jesus is a very popular anal probe.

CPSIA information can be obtained
at www.ICGtesting.com
Printed in the USA
BVHW081928170721
612138BV00003B/342